BEACHCOMBER MOTEL

MEREDITH SUMMERS

CHAPTER ONE

The day was not turning out at all as Jules Whittier had envisioned. The motel that she'd inherited from her grandmother was supposed to be her chance to make up for the complete failure of the last hotel Gram had entrusted her with. But the dilapidated building that stood before her... was it even safe to occupy?

And that wasn't even the worst of it.

Never mind that the Beachcomber Motel, the run-down building that symbolized her second chance at success, looked like it might fall into the ocean at any moment. She'd also just learned that she wouldn't be running the motel alone. Nope, Gram had left equal shares to Jules and her two cousins, Maddie and Gina— the very cousins who had caused her to fail and need that second chance in the first place.

The ocean breeze blew strands of curls around Jules's face, and she pulled them into a clip, trying to keep them in place so they wouldn't frizz as she studied the motel. It was an unusual building. The main portion looked more like an old Victorian with a wide front porch facing the ocean. The porch extended along the back section, where the motel rooms ran in a row. The porch gave the motel an air of interest, and the colorfully painted doors and carved posts set it apart from your regular run-of-the-mill motor inn. Jules tried to see past the chipped paint, missing spindles, and dead plants to envision what it must have looked like in its heyday.

"When was the last time anyone was in that place?" Gina's green eyes narrowed as she gazed across the parking lot, empty except for the three cousins' cars and that of Gram's lawyer.

The girl hadn't stopped scowling since she'd arrived. Jules did not know what she had to scowl about. Last she'd heard, Gina was getting a divorce from her wealthy real estate developer husband, and if the silk blouse she was wearing and candy-apple-red sports car she'd arrived in were any indication, she wasn't hurting for money. She was probably so loaded that she couldn't be bothered with a run-down motel. Jules hoped that was the case. Then she would only have Maddie to get rid of before she could have the place to herself.

"I don't think it's that bad," Maddie said in a

chipper voice, tucking a strand of blond hair behind her ear and smiling. Jules had forgotten how annoyingly upbeat Maddie could be. "A bit of elbow grease and some paint will have it looking good in no time."

Gina snorted. "I think you might be overly optimistic there, cuz. And what about the town? It looks abandoned. Who books a motel in an abandoned town?"

Jules pivoted to look out toward Ocean Street and the town of Shell Cove. From the vantage point of the motel parking lot, they could only see a portion of Main Street, but Gina had a point. There were a few shops open, but several had boarded-up windows and ripped awnings. Window boxes were lined up under the dirty plate-glass windows of some shops, but no flowers could be seen.

"The town has been on a bit of a downswing since they put the new highway in to the west," Steve Rollens, Gram's lawyer, said matter-of-factly.

"Right. So no tourists means no business for the motel." Gina folded her arms over her chest and looked at Jules and Maddie. "I think we should sell."

Jules's heart sank. It was her one chance to make up for what a failure she'd been at running a motel before. She'd even quit her job and sold everything she owned to move there. And, yes, she wanted to do it on her own, without her cousins, but she couldn't afford to buy them out. Not to mention, she'd promised Gram only days before she died that she would bring the motel back to its former glory. Funny thing, Gram had mentioned nothing about including Maddie and Gina in those plans, but Jules couldn't go back on her promise, even if there were a few snags in the plan.

Steve cleared his throat. "Sorry, you can't sell."

Gina swiveled toward him. "What? Why?"

"Rena's will stipulates that you make an earnest attempt to bring the motel back to profit. You need to spend at least a year trying. If you abandon the project, the property will be donated to charity."

"Of course we're not going to abandon the project, Gina," Maddie said. "I mean, look at this gorgeous view! The beach, the ocean."

It was a gorgeous view. The old motel was set atop a cliff with just a few steps down a cement stairway to the sandy beach below. It had a panoramic view of the ocean, and the lapping of the waves on the shore was soothing even from where they stood.

"So you accept the conditions?" Steve asked.

"Of course!" Maddie practically jumped up and down with glee.

"Sure." Jules's stomach roiled with excitement and trepidation.

"I guess." Gina sighed and looked disappointed.

"Good, then I'm to give you these." Steve fished three old brass keys, each hanging from a big blue plastic tag with a faded white Beachcomber Motel stamp, out of his pocket and handed them over. "Good luck, ladies. You're free to go inside anytime."

Maddie glanced from Jules to Gina, her blue eyes sparkling. She linked arms with each of them and dragged them toward the front door. "Come on, you guys. I have a good feeling about this."

Jules exchanged a doubtful look with Gina behind Maddie's back as she let herself be propelled toward the chipped-paint door.

CHAPTER TWO

The interior of the motel wasn't as bad as Maddie had expected. It had obviously been cleaned, the furniture draped in sheets, and everything put away long ago when it had been sealed up. A thin layer of dust had settled on the surfaces, but other than that, it was like stepping back thirty years in time.

The main room was a lobby with a fireplace and a large gathering area. A row of windows on the east side gave a breathtaking view of the ocean. A check-in desk with a white-and-gold-flecked Formica counter sat at one end. A clunky, old computer was on a table behind the desk. A landline phone sat next to the computer, the cord that tethered the receiver curling over the edge.

Beside Maddie, Gina took a deep breath. "At least it doesn't smell moldy, but jeepers this stuff is so outdated."

"Some might consider it charming." Maddie glanced at Jules.

Gram had liked to decorate motels in motifs. One had been rustic with all-natural wood and stone. Another had been Paris-chic with lots of crystals and luxurious furnishings. Jules loved that aspect of Gram's motels. She'd always said she wanted to decorate in some sort of vintage motif, and the Beachcomber came ready with a variety of retro decor.

"It is rather charming." Jules peeked under the corner of one of the drop cloths that covered a big lump of furniture. "Look at all this wicker." She folded the cloth over the top to reveal a set of pristine wicker rocking chairs complete with thick cushions.

"They look comfortable," Maddie said.

"And in great condition." Jules pulled the rest of the tarp off and bent down, her chocolate curls falling over her face as she inspected the chairs.

Maddie tucked her own stick-straight hair behind her ears. What she wouldn't give for perfect curls like Jules.

Jules looked over her shoulder at them, a spark of excitement in her doe-brown eyes. "They're vintage cottage chic if I ever did see it."

"Gram left us a lot to work with," Maddie said. "I know you like to decorate in themes like you did with the other motel we ran."

Jules glanced at her sharply, the spark of excitement

replaced with a look of hurt. Ooops, maybe she shouldn't have mentioned the Surfstone Motel.

The Surfstone had been a cute one-story motel with turquoise shutters. Gram had entrusted the operations of the Surfstone to the three of them when they were in their twenties. They'd messed up though. Maybe they were too young or too inexperienced or too stubborn, but they'd gone bankrupt. All three of them had been equal to blame, but Jules had taken it the hardest.

That had been what caused the rift between the three of them. They hadn't spoken, other than a few nods in passing at various family gatherings, in ten years. But then they were all there. And even if Jules and Gina kept shooting angry looks at each other, Maddie felt fairly confident she could heal that rift. After all, she'd promised Gram she would, and she never went back on her promises.

A bittersweet smile crossed her lips as she thought about that last day with Gram a week before she died. Gram's health had deteriorated, but that day, the look in her eyes was clear, her voice steady, and her grip strong as she took Maddie's hand and made her promise to bring the three cousins back together.

"You're the only one who can do it, Mads." Gram had used the childhood nickname she'd give Maddie. "You always see the best in people and never give up on anything or anyone. Besides, with your sunny attitude, no one can stay mad at you for long."

Gram's faith in Maddie made her sure she could bring them together, and she was excited to make good on her promise. But there was something else. She had a funny feeling that Gram had another reason for wanting her to come to Shell Cove. She just wasn't sure exactly what that was.

"The chairs are nice, but clearly this can't work." Gina gestured around the room. "It's going to take a lot of money to bring this place up to speed, and as far as I know, Gram didn't leave any. Not to mention that town is a ghost town. How are we going to get anyone interested in renting a room?"

Jules and Maddie both stared at Gina for a few beats. Gina had a lot of money, didn't she? Of course, it wouldn't be fair to expect her to foot the bill. Maddie certainly didn't have any, and from what she knew about Jules, she didn't either.

Jules and Gina both looked pretty glum.

Maddie had to do something to turn it around pretty quick. She knew just the thing. Focus on the positive. That always worked. "Everything is clean and in mint condition, so we won't need to do much to get up and running." Maddie held her breath as she flipped the light switch. The lights came on. "Even the lights work. I bet everything works. That eliminates a lot of expense."

The place wasn't that bad. The furniture looked sturdy and clean. The lobby was serviceable. Even the bell over the door had worked when they'd entered. The interior was fine, if a bit outdated, and if they were lucky, they might find that the building itself only needed cosmetic repairs. It was as if Gram had wanted the place to be ready to get up and running right away.

Jules sighed. "I guess that does help. Besides, you heard Mr. Rollens. We're in it now, whether we like it or not. Either we revive it or lose it. And I don't want to lose it. It would be an insult to Gram."

Good. Jules was getting on board. Gina remained silent, her expression indicating she wasn't quite as optimistic. That was okay, though. Maddie was sure she could get her to come around, given time.

"Jules is right. We owe it to Gram to give this a try." Maddie headed toward the door to the right of the check-in desk. "Now let's go check the rest of this place out."

CHAPTER THREE

The longer they poked around in the motel, the more encouraged Jules became. The spacious lobby with its ocean view would be the perfect place to put out fresh-baked muffins or cookies for the guests, giving it the feel of a cozy B and B as opposed to an impersonal roadside motel.

A seating area with couches and chairs was carefully preserved under the tarps. A TV sat on a table along one wall. That would need to be replaced with a newer model, but the overstuffed comfy furniture was timeless. A new, trendy linen slipcover and some colorful pillows would revive it.

Several of the windows had small tables set under them with chairs on either side. Jules could picture people sitting at them to sip coffee or wine and gaze at the ocean or spread out one of the many puzzles that sat in boxes on the bookshelf in the corner.

The lobby would be great for guests to socialize in on rainy days, but she was sure that if the weather was nice, the large porch would be the place to be. Once she decorated that with the cozy wicker furniture Gram had left and some hanging plants, it would be an amazing space. And, since it was just steps from the beach, she was sure it had once been a favorite spot for guests and, hopefully, would be again soon.

As they moved through the space, Jules was already picturing the enhancements she could make to turn it into a retro cottage chic style that would rival those she'd seen in magazines. She had the vision, but how could she pull it off? Somehow they needed to get some money to work with.

The door to the left of the check-in desk led to a small kitchen. It was cute and cozy, and it looked like it belonged back in the 1940s even though Jules was sure the motel wasn't quite that old.

"How old is this place?" Maddie opened a cabinet to reveal it was fully stocked with white ceramic mugs similar to those found in an old diner.

"I'm not sure. Gram had it a long time ago, though. Now that we're walking around, I vaguely remember coming here once when I was really little." Gina trailed her hand along the stainless steel counter, stirring up a bit of dust but nothing that couldn't be cleaned easily. "I think I was about nine or ten."

Jules exchanged a look with Maddie. Gina was the oldest, and Jules was five years younger, but she remembered the summer that Gina's parents split up. It was hard on Gina, and it made sense that Gram would have taken her to the beach. Her heart softened toward her cousin for having to remember a sad time.

"I don't remember ever coming here," Maddie said. "I think Gram must have closed it right after that."

"But why?" Jules asked.

"That summer was kind of a blur, but if I remember correctly, they had moved the main road the year before, and there weren't many tourists coming to town."

Jules's optimism deflated. Even if they could spruce up the motel without spending a lot of money, the problem still remained that no one was coming to Shell Cove.

"That makes sense." Maddie opened another cabinet to reveal stainless steel cookware. "Looks like Gram expected to come back someday, though. She left everything here."

"All the better for us. We're going to need it." Jules opened the fridge and checked the burners on the gas stove. The appliances were older models but in good condition. Maybe Gram had bought them right before she closed the place. Hopefully they would last awhile. She straightened and looked at her cousins. "I'm worried about the situation in town. That might be off-putting to guests."

Maddie wasn't worried though. She was brimming with optimism, as usual. "I don't think that's a big problem. I mean look at the ocean and the beach." She swept her hand toward the window. "All we need to do is push that. Besides, tons of people want relaxing beach vacations without a lot of stressful things pulling them in every direction. This is the perfect setting— nothing to do but sit on the beach and relax."

"That's one way of looking at it." Gina didn't sound convinced, and neither was Jules.

Maddie pulled out a chair and plunked herself down at the round maple kitchen table. Reaching into her tote bag, she pulled out a day planner. Jules almost laughed. She remembered that Maddie was hardly ever without her day planner when they'd managed the Surfstone. Apparently things hadn't changed much.

Maddie flipped the day planner open. "I think we should make a to-do list and assign a time frame and a person to each task." She looked up at Jules and Gina for approval.

"Things haven't changed much with you, have they?" Gina asked.

During their tenure at the Surfstone, Maddie had driven them crazy with her excessive planning and task lists. But Jules had to admit, those things had kept them on track. Not that it had done a lot of good. They'd failed anyway.

Having had enough with the negativity, Jules decided to take a cue from Maddie and think positive. She just hoped Gina wasn't going to drag them down. So far she seemed a lot less than enthusiastic and a little sad. But Maddie had enough optimism for all three of them.

"I suppose we could come up with a list. Then, we'd see what we're up against," Jules said.

Gina shrugged her agreement, and the three of them spent the next hour coming up with a task list. When they were done, Maddie shut the planner and stretched. "I think that's good for now. We have a lot on the list, but I think it's doable."

"But some of this takes money," Jules said.

"And skills. I can assure you I have no idea how to do any of this manual labor." Gina's snotty remark reminded Jules of why they'd grown apart. If she didn't want to help, she didn't have to. Jules and Maddie could do it on their own.

"At least we don't have a mortgage to pay," Jules said. "But there will be electric bills and property taxes. Maybe we can get a loan."

"That's a great idea." Maddie practically squealed. "Why didn't I think of that? The property must be worth a lot. It's right on the ocean. We should be able to leverage that. Great thinking, Jules."

"Thanks." Jules smiled, a glimmer of hope that it might work flickering inside her chest.

Bells tinkled over the front door.

"Hellloooo. Anyone home?" A voice drifted in from the lobby.

The cousins exchanged quizzical looks. Who in the world could that be?

CHAPTER FOUR

Three senior citizens stood in the lobby wearing what looked like their Sunday best. One of them, a short lady with a white pixie cut, was holding an enormous basket.

Jules was unsure of what to do. Who were these ladies? Guests wanting to check in? They hadn't even looked at the rooms yet and doubted any of them would be ready for people to stay in.

Maddie stepped forward to greet them. "Hi, welcome to the Beachcomber Motel. How can I help you?"

"You must be Maddie," said the taller one with a halo of gray curly hair on top of her head and intelligent blue eyes that reminded her of Gram.

"I am." Maddie looked bemused. "And you are?"

"Welcome wagon. Your grandmother told us you'd

be coming." Pixie Haircut thrust the basket toward them. "We brought you some goodies."

"Thank you." Maddie took the basket. "So you were friends of our grandmother?"

"Yep." The third lady, who was medium height with a spikey haircut and an abrupt demeanor, gestured around the room. "We made sure the lights were on for you."

"And we had the cleaning service come in to do the motel, and we had a room prepared for each of you." The tall one looked at the windowsill and frowned. "Sorry if it's a little dusty. We don't exactly have top-notch cleaning people in town anymore."

"But that's going to change." Pixie Haircut made a face. "Oh, how forgetful of us. We haven't even introduced ourselves. I'm Pearl Flannery."

The tall one came forward. "And I'm Rose Wisnewski."

"Leena McCain," the other woman said simply.

Jules got the impression she wasn't one to waste words.

The girls introduced themselves, though the ladies seemed to know who each of them was anyway.

"How nice of you to come." Jules peered into the basket. It was loaded with goodies: bread, pasta, peanut butter, even milk.

"Would you like to come into the kitchen for some tea?" Maddie asked.

The three ladies exchanged a glance.

"We'd love to." Rose looked around the room, a wistful smile on her face. "We haven't been in here in nearly thirty years."

"Really? You guys have lived in town all this time?"

"Yes, we were good friends with your grandmother and want to extend our condolences for her passing," Pearl said.

"Thank you," all three of them murmured.

In the kitchen, Jules rummaged through the basket and broke out some shortbread cookies that looked homemade while Gina made the tea.

"Rose made the cookies. They're her specialty." Pearl took a crystal plate out of the cupboard and arranged the cookies on it then grabbed napkins from the basket and mugs and silverware from the cupboard and drawers. Apparently she was familiar with where things were kept in the kitchen.

"Did you guys spend a lot of time in here with Gram?" Jules asked.

"Oh yes. The four of us were always together back in the day," Rose said.

"We're going to miss her terribly," Pearl added.

"So, what do you girls plan to do with the motel?" Leena asked bluntly.

"We were just talking about that. Gram's will states that we have to try to make a go of it, and I think we've agreed." Jules glanced at her cousins.

Maddie nodded enthusiastically.

Gina shrugged.

"We were just making a plan." Maddie pointed to the day planner that lay open on the table.

"A day planner. That's very organized of you." Rose looked at Maddie over the rim of her mug. "We could really use someone like you here."

Jules frowned. What did they mean by here? At the motel? Maddie was already at the motel.

"The problem is…" Gina's tone dripped with pessimism. "We don't have any money to fix up the hotel, and the town is a ghost town."

The welcome-wagon ladies seemed to consider that. "That may be true, but we have an idea for the town. It will be easy to bring the town back. All we need is a bit of interest to bring tourists."

"As you can see, the location is pristine." Rose gestured toward the windows and the ocean beyond.

"It used to be a bustling town," Pearl added.

"Back in your grandmother's day, this hotel was hopping." Leena picked another cookie from the plate.

"And we want to help you bring it back to the way it used to be. Your grandmother wanted that." Rose's tone had a note of finality, as if they had no other choice.

"And for the money, we know someone down at the Shell Cove bank, and it might be a good idea to consider a loan," Pearl said.

"We were just taking about that," Jules said.

"That leaves the question of bringing tourists back to town." Leena tapped at the day planner. "You seem very organized. Maybe we could use your skills to help with planning that, if you don't mind."

Maddie's eyes shone. "Mind? I'd love it. When do we start?"

"First, let's take care of the issues with the motel. I can introduce one of you to our contact at the bank and put in a good word if you want," Pearl said.

Gina and Maddie looked at Jules. At the Surfstone, she'd always been the one to handle finances and book-keeping.

"I'll do it," Jules said.

Rose took her mug to the sink. "Good. We'll swing by to pick you up tomorrow at nine?"

They escorted the ladies out and watched them get into an old Dodge Dart.

Pearl rolled down her window to talk to them. "Enjoy your rooms. They're rooms nine, ten, and eleven. We hope Ellie, the cleaner, has them made up to your satisfaction."

The three cousins watched them drive off.

"At least we have a little bit of help from someone in town," Maddie said. "And it was nice of them to have the place cleaned and to bring the basket of food."

Jules yawned. "Not to mention getting rooms set up for us. Let's go check them out. It's been a long day, and I'm beat."

Rose glanced in her rearview mirror as she drove away from the motel. "I think that went well, don't you?"

In the passenger seat, Pearl nodded. "They are a lot more willing to get the motel going than I thought they would be. Especially Maddie. Rena was right about her. She does have an aptitude for organization."

"Maybe Gina wasn't so hot on the idea," Leena said from the back.

"Rena said Gina might be a bit of trouble. Rena seemed to think Gina's lost her way."

"Maddie is exactly what we need for the town planner job, but I think you might be rushing her a bit, Rose. Remember, we agreed to go slowly." Pearl glanced at her friend. "We don't want her to get spooked and bolt."

"Point taken," Rose said. "I just got excited."

"I'm sure everything will work out. I hope the bank will see fit to give them a loan," Pearl said. "You know how Henry can be."

"That's why we're not taking her to Henry. We're going to take her to Nick." Rose smiled slyly. "I think she and Nick will get along just great."

Pearl narrowed her eyes at Rose. "Are you trying to fix them up?"

"No, but if it works out that way…"

Leena perked up in the back seat. "Sounds like this is ripe for a bet."

The three were known to place wagers among themselves on certain topics.

Pearl shrugged. "Maybe. If Henry doesn't screw things up. You know he still has a grudge against Rena after all these years."

Rose pressed her lips together. "I never really understood what that was about. They were such good friends."

Leena sat back in the seat. "That was a long time ago."

"Yes, well, better days are ahead for us and for the town," Pearl said.

Leena sighed. "I just hope those girls are up for the challenge. Rena said she'd send us some angels to help with the town, but judging by what I saw tonight, we might have our work cut out for us."

CHAPTER FIVE

The room was nicer than Gina had expected. Not Hyatt Regency nice and nothing like the expensive luxury hotels she was used to—or rather, had been used to. That was all in the past. She might never be able to afford those hotels again.

The room was spacious, with a king-size bed and a large window overlooking the ocean. The brown-and-orange color scheme was a bit outdated, but she supposed that had been popular in the 1980s when the hotel was last open. Despite the age of the motel, the room showed only minimal signs of wear and tear. Perhaps Gram had updated it shortly before she was forced to close.

At least the room didn't smell moldy, she thought as she opened the window and breathed the salty sea air.

And the view was spectacular. The old place did have a few things going for it.

She collapsed onto the bed. It was surprisingly comfortable. But the nonmoldy room and comfortable bed didn't make her feel much better as she checked her email to find only spam. She'd reached out to some of her and her ex-husband's old friends to see if any one of them had heard from her husband, Hugh, but so far no luck.

She threw the phone on the bed in disgust. The entire world, including Maddie and Jules, thought she was getting a divorce, but the truth was that Hugh had disappeared along with their sizable bank account and his young secretary, Holly.

That had been almost six months ago, and Gina had no idea where he was. Gina had visions of him and a bikini-clad Holly on a tropical island. Those visions had hurt at first, but at that point she couldn't care less about Hugh or where he was. The only problem was that without knowing his whereabouts, she couldn't very well serve him with divorce papers. Oh, and the money, that was a problem, too, because he'd taken it all, and she had no idea how to get her half back.

She could tell that her cousins thought she was rolling in money, but she was completely broke. It was proving to be quite an adjustment.

Her phone pinged, and she grabbed it off the bed. The message wasn't about Hugh; it was her neighbor,

Melissa. Mel was back in Beacon Hill, an exclusive section of Boston where she'd lived with Hugh. Mel didn't know about Hugh's disappearance either. She thought they were simply getting divorced and Gina was looking to downsize. Mel was actively searching the condo listings for Gina and kept messaging her with potential units.

Thankfully Gina's name had been the only one on the mortgage and title of the heavily mortgaged home she'd shared with Hugh, so she could sell it without him being present. Maybe his insistence on her name being the only one associated with the home should have been a clue, but she'd been blinded by his charm. She'd been lucky to get out of the home without owing money. But she had nothing to put down on a new condo, and she'd had to keep putting Mel off by claiming the ones Mel presented to her were not suitable. Hopefully if she held off long enough, she would figure out a way to recover the money Hugh had stolen.

She could figure that out, couldn't she? Hugh's voice rang in her head, evaporating her confidence.

"It's a good thing we have money. You don't really have many skills," he'd said.

When he'd said that, she'd thought it oddly insulting, but then he'd laughed that charming, dimple-producing laugh, and she'd figured he was just kidding. But she did have skills, didn't she? Maybe she'd never had a chance to showcase them with Hugh. She'd spend most of her time staging the high-end properties that Hugh sold. He'd said she had a knack for furniture placement and coordinating accessories.

Maybe Hugh had been right. She didn't have the skills to find him or her money. That was for sure.

Glancing around the room, she found herself automatically staging it. It needed an upgrade, but it wouldn't take much. Maybe move some things around, get some new, coordinating bedding, a new rug, shower curtains and some rolled-up towels in the bathrooms to give it a spa effect. New paint was a must. But she was getting ahead of herself. She wasn't going to be there long enough to decorate the place.

She hefted her suitcase onto the bed and started to unpack. The room actually had a decent closet and wooden hangers. The bureau drawers opened smoothly, but the bulky bureau took up a lot of room. Did motel guests really need a big bureau? Maybe a smaller one built into the closet would open up the space for a nice chair.

But just because the motel had wooden hangers and possibilities didn't mean she would be staying. Nope, renovating a motel was not for her, especially not with her cousins. They were the last people she wanted to work with, particularly Jules. She and Maddie hadn't exactly proven they were up for the job before. The failure at the Surfstone motel had done a number on Gina's confidence, even though it was mostly all their fault. That, if nothing else, was the reason she would be leaving the Beachcomber as soon as possible.

She'd made Gram a deathbed promise that she would come there, and she'd fulfilled that promise. Luckily, she hadn't promised how long she would stay. And as for her promise to enjoy the simple things... well, what did that even mean?

CHAPTER SIX

*M*addie breezed into the kitchen early the next morning. She'd been pleasantly surprised at the condition of her room. She'd slept hard and awakened optimistic about the future of the motel.

But first, coffee.

"Where is the coffee maker?" she muttered as she scoured the room, looking for the Keurig and K-Cup setup she was used to at home.

She didn't find a Keurig. All she found was an old-fashioned coffee maker with a basket and a pot. It was white with a yellow gingham decal across the top. It had a name, too—Mr. Coffee.

"Okay, Mr. Coffee, let's see if I can figure you out." She rummaged in the basket the welcome-wagon ladies had given her and found coffee filters and ground coffee. But she couldn't figure out how to get the thing working, no matter how hard she fiddled with it. Maddie had many strong suits, but understanding gadgets and technology was not one.

"Fine. I can hold off on the coffee." Frustrated with the machine, she sat at the table, took a notebook out of her purse, and set it beside her open day planner. First, she needed to figure out what jobs absolutely had to be done at the hotel, then she could schedule the dates. There were plenty of things they could do on their own, and if the loan came through, she could move on to bigger projects. She had no idea how much they might get for a loan, and it was important to prioritize. Maddie was very good at prioritizing.

But how was she going to get Jules and Gina to work together? She'd already sensed the tension between them. She'd hoped they would have some cousin bonding time the night before, after the welcome-wagon ladies left, but both Jules and Gina had said they were too tired and hurried off to their rooms without even saying good night to each other.

No worries; Maddie could work on that. At least they were talking to each other. Well, not actually talking, but at least they weren't fighting.

Looking down at the calendar, she felt a thrill of excitement. There was nothing Maddie liked more than to plan things, and soon all the empty squares would be filled in with tasks that would take them one step closer to a profitable motel. It gave her a sense of purpose, and crossing them off would give her a sense of accomplishment.

"I don't smell any coffee." Gina appeared in the doorway, yawning. Her brown hair was tussled, and she had a look of severe caffeine deprivation in her eyes.

Maddie gestured toward the Mr. Coffee, who seemed to mock her with his gleaming glass coffeepot and cheery yellow decor. "I couldn't figure out how to work that thing."

Gina raised a brow at her. "Seriously?"

Maddie shrugged. "Well, you know me. I'm not good with these things."

Gina shuffled over to the machine and inspected it. "I think the lid that goes over the pot is missing." She rummaged around in the drawers, pulling out various utensils, the last being an old wooden rolling pin with a design embedded in it.

Gina turned and held it out. "Do you remember that from Gram? She used to make those fancy pies with it. Tried to teach me a few times."

Memories of Gram made Maddie smile. Gram always tried to spend a lot of time with them. Since Gina was older, they hadn't done much together with their grandmother. Apparently Gina remembered the rolling pin, but with Maddie, it was cookies. She'd loved

Gram's shortbread cookies. "She always had the best way of making the simplest things so enjoyable and important."

Gina's gaze flicked to Maddie, a look of surprise and longing in her eyes that put Maddie off-balance.

"Is something wrong?" Maddie asked.

Gina's expression went back to its previous one of annoyance. "No. You're right. Gram was great. Now go back to your planning, and leave me alone so I can figure out how to get this coffee going."

GINA PUT THE LID ON THE COFFEEPOT AND POURED water into the machine. Her gaze drifted to the rolling pin, her mind swirling with memories of her grandmother. Gram had tried to teach her to make pies with that very pin. She'd treasured those times alone with Gram.

Gram had made her promise to enjoy the simple things, but surely she didn't mean pies.

Maddie had mentioned that Gram made the simplest things seem important, and Gram knew that Gina hadn't done any of her own cooking, cleaning, or much of anything else in the past several years. She'd had people to do all those things for her. Of course, now she would have to learn to do them for herself.

She tapped the counter, impatient for the coffee to brew, while Maddie twittered away about the various projects they would need to consider if they wanted the motel to be successful.

Gina tried to keep from strangling her. If the girl would just wait until she had some caffeine, she might be better able to withstand the chattering.

Finally, the coffee was done, and Gina poured a mug for both of them. She put Maddie's on the table and leaned against the counter, closing her eyes as she took the first delicious sip.

Gina opened her eyes just in time to see Jules walk in. Great. Now she would have to deal with both of them. She moved away from the coffee machine and let Jules pour her own.

"Did you both sleep well? The rooms are actually very cozy." Maddie looked as bright as a bunny sitting at the table. How could the girl be so put together first thing in the morning? But then she'd always been like that, much to Gina's annoyance.

"I did." Jules pulled the milk out of the fridge and poured a generous amount into her coffee. It was practically a milkshake. Gina liked hers black. They couldn't even agree on how to drink coffee. "I was afraid they'd need all kinds of repairs, but mine was okay. What about you guys?"

Jules glanced at Gina out of the corner of her eye,

looking away quickly when their eyes met. So Jules didn't even want to look her in the eye? That figured. It would be just like Jules to still hold a grudge. Oh well, hopefully she wouldn't be there long enough to let that old wound fester.

"Mine was adequate. I mean, it's not the Taj Mahal, but it's okay for a beach motel. A little outdated." Gina sipped her coffee.

"But serviceable," Maddie said. "And if we get a loan, then we can update them."

"We'll know about that today." Jules glanced out the window. "The welcome-wagon ladies should be here any minute."

"I bet it won't cost much to spruce up the rooms," Gina ventured.

"I agree. I was picturing maybe some sea-themed comforters and throw pillows. You know, like seahorses in one room, shells in another, starfish in another."

Jules's excitement grated on Gina's nerves. Maybe she needed more coffee, or maybe it was because Jules always plowed over Gina's ideas with her own.

"Really? All the hotels have white bedding now. It looks chic and is easy because it's the same for every room." Gina wondered why she'd said anything.

Jules made a face. "But we don't want to be like the other hotels. We want a theme. That's what Gram always had."

"Well, I don't think we have enough money for a

theme. White is crisp and easy." Gina felt herself getting angry. It was always the same thing with Jules, her way or the highway. That was exactly what had happened before and, in Gina's opinion, was one of the reasons why they'd gone under at the Surfstone.

Jules was getting angry too. She crossed her arms over her chest. "We're not sacrificing quality and our brand to save some money. Those are the kinds of things that people will talk about to their friends, and that brings more business into the motel." She huffed.

Gina took a deep breath, ready for the usual argument.

"You guys, we can do both! Jules is really good at picking out the items, and, Gina, you're good at figuring out where to put them." Maddie, ever the referee, tried to smooth things over. "Let's not argue about it now. We don't even know what we have to work with. Speaking of which, I made a list of some tasks. I think we should prioritize them. A lot of them will just require elbow grease, and we can get started right away."

Elbow grease? Gina wasn't used to that. She hadn't done much manual labor in years. She wasn't really good at it. Just like Hugh had said, she didn't have many skills. But still, Maddie had just said she was good at figuring out how to arrange rooms. Was that true, or had Maddie just said that to stop the argument from escalating?

It was best to just play along. Hopefully she wouldn't

be there long enough to have to do any of the work. She was much better at luncheons and day spas, not painting or kitchen work. Her eyes strayed to the rolling pin. But since she didn't have the money for luncheons and day spas, it might not hurt to try her hand at some more practical endeavors.

CHAPTER SEVEN

Jules sat in the passenger seat of Rose's old Dodge Dart. She'd offered to ride in the back, but the welcome-wagon ladies had insisted that guests sat in the front.

Rose, Pearl, and Leena were dressed more casually that day in capri pants and cotton shirts. It was a hot day, and the sun beating through the window heated up the car, but the older ladies seemed to enjoy the warm temperature, so Jules didn't ask Rose to blast the air conditioning.

As they drove down Main Street, Rose pointed out the various businesses.

"This one over here is Saltwater Sweets shop. That's owned by Deena Walters. Been in her family for generations." Rose pointed to one of the few shops that was open.

Jules could see someone inside making a purchase at an old-fashioned cash register. The window had a haphazard display of chocolates, and the exterior looked like it needed some attention.

"Poor Deena. She lost her husband a few years back, and as you can see, the business has been going to ruin." Leena pressed her lips together and shook her head.

"I heard she got a new boyfriend." Pearl sounded optimistic.

Rose glanced at her in the rearview mirror. "Really? I saw her at the market with a tall, thin guy. She was smiling. Guess that must be him."

Pearl nodded. "I did too. They seemed quite smitten with each other. Though there may be trouble with her daughter, Samantha."

Leena's left brow quirked up. "What kind of trouble?"

Pearl waved her hand. "Oh, you know, Samantha doesn't trust the new guy. Same stuff everyone goes through at our age. But I heard he might invest in the business, so he can't be that bad."

"You'd think Samantha would be grateful about that." Rose turned to Jules. "The business has been going downhill a bit, like most of the stores here."

"They're not that bad though, right, Jules?" Pearl asked. "The market still looks nice, and the garden store down at the end is bursting with lush plants."

"You're right. It's not quite as bad as I thought at first," Jules said. Even though some businesses were boarded up, many of them were still open. A lot of them did need a fresh coat of paint and new awnings. She felt hopeful that there was potential. "Maybe some flowers in the window boxes under the shop windows and the planters on the street would help."

"I think we can make a lot of improvements," Rose said. "Cassie at the coffee shop was just saying that the other day."

Jules looked in the direction Rose pointed to see a cute little coffee shop. It had bistro tables set outside and, unlike many of the other businesses, looked as clean as a whistle with a bright-turquoise awning, sparkling windows, and a line of customers inside.

"She does quite a business," Leena said. "Makes the best latte in the county."

"But what about the businesses that are boarded up? What happened to them?" Jules asked.

"Those are the ones that relied on tourists. Others, like the coffee shop, the restaurants, and the garden center, can rely on business from the folks in town. Salt-water Sweets is lucky because people have been coming from all over for their candy for generations, so they get some outside tourist traffic."

"And the corner diner down on Ocean Ave. gets business from the fishermen that frequent the pier."

Leena gestured toward the long wooden pier that jutted out from the town beach.

There were several men fishing from the end of the pier and what looked like an abandoned store just on the edge of the pier near the parking lot.

"What's that?" asked Jules.

Rose sighed. "Used to be Shell Cove Donuts. They made dozens of flavors. People would come from all over for the variety. But when the tourist trade dried up, they had to close."

"They were set up for high volume. Couldn't survive on the dribs and drabs from the town and the people that come to fish," Leena added.

"But no worries," Pearl said. "We have a plan. With the hotel being renovated now, we can bring in tourists. In fact, we're having a town meeting with the business owners to make a plan."

Jules swiveled in her seat. "A meeting?"

"Yeah, you know, like a town meeting. We can discuss how to revitalize the town."

"I suppose that could be good." Jules thought it was a great idea. She needed the town to be revitalized if they were going to get guests at the motel. "I'm sure Maddie will like that."

"Indeed, she can bring her day planner and schedule things for us."

"It will be a potluck supper, of course," Rose said.

"Potluck supper?" Jules had been picturing something a little more formal, like maybe in the town hall with gavels to call the meeting to order and podiums to speak at. But maybe in small towns like Shell Cove they did things differently.

"Yes, that's how we've always done things. Well, when we used to have meetings back in the day," Rose said. "I've always found there is a much better turnout when food is involved."

"Uh-huh, and we'll all bring our signature dishes, of course." Pearl was practically jumping up and down with excitement.

"Signature dishes?" Jules could barely boil water, and she knew Gina and Maddie weren't any better at it. Would they be expected to bring a signature dish?

"Of course!" Leena said. "Everyone has a signature dish. Mine is deviled eggs. Rose makes the most unusual coleslaw. Deena brings chocolate, naturally. And your grandmother used to bring the best pies."

"She did make good pies." Jules remembered that her grandmother would make elaborate pies for every family gathering. She'd tried to teach Jules how to do it once, but that had been a disaster. Pie crust required too much patience for Jules's liking. She doubted she could bring a pie to the town meeting. "I'll have to see what we can do. We aren't really—really set up at the motel for baking or anything."

"Oh, I'm sure you'll figure something out," Pearl said as Rose parked in front of a formal-looking white building. The black sign with gold lettering identified it as the Mariner's Bank, Shell Cove Branch.

"Do you see Henry in there?" Rose whispered to the ladies in the back seat.

They craned their necks. "I don't think he's there. The coast is clear."

Jules got a bad feeling. "Who is Henry?"

"Oh, don't worry about him, dear. He's just an old curmudgeon. He's the president of the bank, but you won't have to deal with him. He's semiretired. I was going to bring you in to meet his grandson, Nick. He's much nicer." Rose opened the door and turned to Jules. "Come on. I'll take you in to meet him."

CHAPTER EIGHT

The interior of the Shell Cove bank looked much as it would have looked eighty years ago. Marble floor, fluted columns, tellers behind gold-barred windows.

Rose's footsteps echoed on the floor as she led Jules across the empty lobby to a row of mahogany-desked offices.

Only one of them was occupied, and the man sitting behind the desk stood as they approached. He had dark hair that curled around the collar of his starched white dress shirt, whiskey-brown eyes, a tanned face, and an easy smile. "Rose, how nice to see you."

His gaze drifted to Jules, causing a minor flutter in her chest. Very minor. She had no business getting flut-tery about a stranger. She had work to do, and flutters would only get in the way of that.

"Nick, this is Jules Whittier. She inherited the Beachcomber." Rose glanced behind them, as if avoiding someone, which was odd since they appeared to be the only people there.

"Oh? That's great." He came out from behind the desk to shake her hand. He was tall, probably over six feet, and smelled like spices, not in an unpleasant way either. "Nice to meet you. Are you going to try to open it again?"

"Yes." Much to Jules's horror, her voice came out a little breathless. She cleared her throat. "That's why I'm here. I'd like to see about a loan."

"Oh, great. Have a seat." Nick gestured to the chair situated in front of the desk. "I can get a chair for you, Rose."

"Oh, no." Rose was already backing out of the office, glancing nervously down the row of other offices. "I'll leave you to it. I'll be out waiting in the car, Jules."

Nick went back behind the desk. "It seems like a big task to open the motel. It's been closed awhile. Must be a lot of work involved."

"It is, but my cousins are helping. We were hoping, since Gram didn't owe money on it, we could use the property for collateral."

Nick nodded as he typed into the computer. She noticed he had big hands, broad shoulders too. He didn't look like a guy who would work in a bank, more like a sports player. She found herself wondering what his story was.

"… once we do a credit check."

"Huh? Oh, credit check. Yes, that will be fine." Jules gnawed her bottom lip. Her credit wasn't that good. Hopefully Maddie and Gina were doing better in that department. Gina must be. She was rich.

"I'll need all three of you to fill it out if you all want to be on the loan." The printer whirred to life behind him.

"Of course." Anxiety wormed its way into Jules's thoughts. What if their bad credit ruined their chances of getting a loan? "So you think it will be a problem? I don't even know how much we'll need, really."

"Problem? No, I don't think so. Of course we'll have to send the forms through and see what happens. I'm sure it will be fine." Nick's warm brown gaze was reassuring.

Nick swiveled in his chair and pulled the papers off the printer.

Jules sat back and smiled, her stomach in knots. Of course Nick was right. The loan would go through. It had to, because they had no other way to bring the motel up to speed.

Nick slid the papers across his desk to Jules. He sensed she was nervous and wanted to put her at ease. She seemed vulnerable somehow, and it spoke to his heart. Not to mention she was one of the most beautiful girls he'd ever seen, with those dark curls cascading past her shoulders like satin ribbons and the depth in her almond-shaped brown eyes that hinted she was more than just a pretty face.

He was embarrassed to admit that he'd quickly glanced at her left hand. No ring. That was good. But he was getting ahead of himself. Business first. The lady wanted a loan, and he was happy to oblige.

"This page just gives us permission to check your credit. I'll need all three of your signatures here." Nick leaned across the desk to put his finger on the signature line and caught a whiff of vanilla. He sat down and pushed his chair back a tad. It would be easier to keep his mind on business that way.

"Okay." She pulled the paper closer to read it.

"Do you have a business entity set up?"

She glanced up. "Good question. We haven't talked about that. We all just arrived yesterday and haven't had much of a chance to discuss the project."

"You'll probably want to set one up. I can get you started with our premium business account, and when you get the legal paperwork done, we can transfer it."

"That sounds great." The grateful look Jules gave

him made him glad that he'd suggested it. "I'll have to talk to my cousins."

"Of course. So you'll be staying in town to run the motel?" Nick blurted that last part.

"Yes. I've run a motel before. In fact, the three of us have."

Jules looked uncomfortable about that revelation, so Nick didn't ask further. Instead he continued to explain each aspect of the loan application, taking a lot longer than he did with any other loan customer.

Not that he'd had many loan customers lately. Over the past few years, fewer and fewer people had been able to qualify for a loan. Nick was afraid the town was slowly going even further downhill, and it killed him to see the townsfolk that he'd known his whole life draining their savings just to keep their businesses open so they could break even.

Could reviving the Beachcomber revive the town? Nick certainly hoped so. He loved his town and would like nothing more than to see it thrive again, to come in and see the lobby full of people cashing checks and depositing money. He bet Gramps would like that too. And, more than anything, Nick wanted to see Gramps happy again.

Nick wasn't sure when Gramps had turned into a crotchety old man. He'd been a happy man once, before Gram died. Gramps had grieved for a long time, and Nick thought someone else had made him happy for a while, but that wasn't meant to be, and Gramps had sunk even deeper into sadness.

Maybe if the town was revived, even a little, that would bring the old Gramps back.

CHAPTER NINE

*M*addie was standing outside the Beachcomber, making notes about the exterior maintenance they needed to do, when the welcome-wagon ladies dropped Jules off.

"How did it go at the bank?" Maddie noticed Jules flush slightly at the question. Weird.

"Good. I brought back this loan paperwork to fill out. Didn't sound like it would be a big problem to get one." Jules held up a stack of papers, glancing at the clipboard in Maddie's hands. "What are you doing?"

"Trying to come up with a plan. I don't think the motel's condition is as bad as we thought. See here." Maddie pointed to the wide front porch. "We just need to do some scraping and painting and replace a few spindles. That's easy and doesn't cost a lot."

"And the rest of it?" Jules glanced down the long

line of motel room doors and tried to calculate how much it would cost to update the rooms.

"That might take a bit more money," Maddie admitted. She didn't mention that there could also be hidden damage that might require costly repairs—things like old wiring, outdated plumbing, and the roof. For the time being, the cosmetic changes were all they could tackle.

"Maybe we can do the rooms a few at a time. That way we can start booking a few guests sooner to get some money flowing. Speaking of which, Rose mentioned something about a town meeting to discuss bringing tourists back to the town," Jules said. "We're invited."

"That sounds like a good idea." Maddie glanced at the ocean. "We have a lot to talk about, and we haven't even checked out the beach yet. Let's drop the forms in the kitchen and see if Gina wants to go for a walk so we can talk about our strategy."

Gina was sitting at the table, her head bent over her phone, which she abruptly put away as soon as they walked in. She looked a little guilty, but Maddie couldn't imagine about what.

"We're going to walk the beach and talk about the plan for the motel," Maddie said.

Gina looked less than enthused but went along with them anyway.

On the beach, they slipped off their shoes. Maddie

dug her toes into the warm sand and took a deep breath. "I can't believe I haven't been down here yet!"

"I know, right? It's amazing." Jules shaded her eyes, gazing out into the ocean.

The low tide had created a wide strip of wet sand between them and the waves. One end of the beach had an outcropping of rocks, which Maddie imagined housed starfish, snails, crabs, and maybe even a sea urchin. She made a mental note to check that out later. In the other direction, the beach stretched for miles.

The sound of the surf was soothing, the sun glinting off the cobalt water mesmerizing, and the scent of the sea air therapeutic. Even Gina had a smile on her face.

"Let's go down by the water. I bet it's refreshingly cold." Jules ran toward the water's edge, and Maddie and Gina followed.

Even on the hottest summer day, the Atlantic Ocean in Maine was frigid. That day was no exception. Jules rushed right in up to midcalf, but Maddie dipped her toes in an inch at a time, finally letting the waves rush over her feet. Her toes were numb after a minute, but it still felt good.

They started walking, their feet splashing in the foamy edge of the water as they followed a group of sandpipers down the beach.

"Remember all the times Gram took us to the beach?" Maddie had fond memories of family beach days with Jules, Gina, and several of their other cousins.

Though Gina was a bit older and usually wanted to lie on the beach towel and work on her tan, Maddie remembered making sandcastles and splashing in the water with Jules. She hoped the memories would remind Jules and Gina about what was really important and help bring them closer.

"Those were good times," Jules said. "I don't spend nearly as much time at the beach anymore. Even when I lived in Lobster Bay. I guess I was too busy working."

"Ditto. Guess we need to remember to make time to enjoy things." Maddie turned to Gina. "What about you, Gina?"

Gina frowned. "I didn't live near the beach."

It sounded like that was the extent of Gina's small talk, so Maddie steered the conversation toward business. "Jules brought home the application from the bank."

"Oh, great," Gina said.

"The guy there, Nick, asked about a business entity," Jules said. "I'm not sure if Gram had one or if we need to create something."

"Oh, good thinking!" Maddie couldn't believe she hadn't thought of that. "I'll talk to Steve and find out what the best thing is. We're running a business now and have to act as such. We can still move ahead with some projects, though."

Maddie told them about the projects she thought they should do first—sprucing up the exterior of the motel, scraping, painting, landscaping, and redoing the rooms a few at a time, as Jules had suggested. "The best part is we can do most of this ourselves. It won't cost a lot and will make a big impact. Remember, the goal is to get tourists to book rooms right away."

Gina's frown deepened. "What tourists? I don't think there are any."

Jules sighed. She was walking on Maddie's right, and Gina was on Maddie's left, as if the two were using Maddie as some sort of buffer. Jules leaned over to look across Maddie at her cousin. "You don't need to be so negative. The town is working on getting tourists."

Gina's eyes flashed. "I wasn't being negative. I was being practical. And besides, what great plan does the town have now, and why haven't they used it to bring in tourists before?"

"We'll have to wait and see what the plan is. I get the impression they were waiting for the Beachcomber to open up before doing anything." Jules told Gina about the town meeting and potluck. "We're expected to bring a signature dish. Do either of you have one?"

Gina snorted. "You mean like cook something?"

Maddie could sense the tension starting to simmer between her cousins. She would have to tamp it down with her positive attitude. "I think it would be great if they have some ideas. We need tourists in town to make this work. As for the signature dish… well… I guess we can come up with something."

"Okay, you like being in charge of stuff, so you can be in charge of the signature dish, Mads," Jules said.

Maddie smiled at the use of her childhood nickname. The three of them had been close back then, and she felt that the use of the name was a sign that they were slowly getting back to that. It hadn't even been two days yet, but so far, she'd been pleasantly surprised that neither Jules nor Gina had shown animosity toward her.

Of course it made sense because neither of them had really been that mad at her when they'd parted ways after the Surfstone, but she'd expected a colder reception. She still had her work cut out for her when it came to Jules and Gina, but she was starting to see signs that she could accomplish that and make good on her promise to Gram.

"Rose said that Gram always brought pies," Jules said.

"That's interesting. Gina found a rolling pin in the kitchen." Maddie glanced at Gina.

She had a thoughtful look on her face.

"Didn't you say you used to make pies with Gram?"

Gina's expression snapped back into a scowl. "I said she tried to teach me when I was a kid. I was no good at it then, and I'm sure as heck not going to be any better at it now."

CHAPTER TEN

*N*ick stood in the lobby looking down the street after Jules left. The boarded-up shops really bothered him. Those were family businesses, hopes and dreams. But if Jules brought the motel back to life, maybe those businesses could open again. He had a feeling they were on the verge of something hopeful and positive. And not just for the town. Maybe for himself too.

Gramps came up beside him. "Who was that girl?"

"Jules Whittier."

Gramps's normal scowl deepened. "Whittier? What did she want?"

"A loan. I guess she and her cousins inherited the Beachcomber, and they want to fix it up."

"A loan for a motel here in this town?" Gramps

barked out a laugh. "That doesn't sound like a good investment for the bank."

Nick's gut tightened. "What do you mean? We need to service more loans. You said so yourself."

"Yeah, but this one is too risky. Who is going to stay at that old, broken-down motel?"

Gramps had raised his voice a bit, and Josie, the teller, glanced over at them. Nick took his arm and led him a few feet down the private hallway where Gramps's office was.

"That's the point of the loan, to renovate it so people will want to go there."

"Ack! You believe that girl?" Gramps looked like he'd eaten a lemon.

Did he know something about Jules? "Why wouldn't I believe her? Do you know her?"

"I know her kind. Knew her grandmother. Those Whittiers are bad news, and I don't want anything to do with them." Gramps jerked his arm away and continued toward his office, his feet shuffling on the red carpet runner that covered the marble floor.

Nick's heart grew heavy as he watched Gramps walk away. Until recently, Gramps had had a spring in his step, but the past few years he'd aged so much. It took him longer to get around anymore, and Nick heard him wincing with pain sometimes. Nick couldn't imagine life without Gramps. The thought was too horrible. He'd idolized the man since he was a small child, and Gramps had been very good to him. The two had been almost inseparable since Nick was old enough to walk.

But still, Gramps was wrong about it. Nick knew it in his gut.

Nick followed him down the hall. "What do you mean? You're not going to approve the loan just because of who she is?"

"Nope, that's only part of it. The other part is that it's a bad investment for the bank."

"But the property itself must be worth millions. It's right on the ocean," Nick argued.

Gramps gave him a look, and Nick remembered how run-down the motel was.

"Okay, maybe hundreds of thousands. Much more than what we would lend."

"What is the bank going to do with a motel on the ocean?" Gramps stopped at his office door and turned to Nick. "We're in the business of money, not real estate."

Good question. "I guess we would sell it off if they defaulted, but I have a good feeling about this. I don't think they will default. And it could really help the town."

"The town?" Henry gestured toward the sad-looking Main Street beyond the window. "No one comes here anymore. There's no one to rent rooms in the motel. Therefore, the motel won't make an income.

Therefore, they won't be able to pay back the loan, and therefore, the bank won't be able to sell it. We'll be stuck."

Nick remained silent. He had a million arguments running around in his head, but he could tell Gramps wouldn't listen to any of them.

Gramps's expression softened. "I'm sorry, son. It's too risky. Take my advice, and don't let a pretty face sway you."

Gramps turned away and went into his office. "We're not approving the loan, and that's final."

Nick stood in the doorway and watched his grandfather plop into the chair behind his desk. He never went against Gramps's wishes. Ever. But his heart was telling him that Gramps was wrong. And it wasn't just because he didn't want to disappoint Jules. He loved his town and wanted do whatever he could to help it prosper. The Beachcomber Motel could change everything for Shell Cove. There had to be a way to get that loan without Gramps's approval, and Nick was going to find it.

CHAPTER ELEVEN

That night in the kitchen, Gina lifted the rolling pin, her fingertips tracing the smooth wood worn from decades of use. Gram had a few of these, each with different patterns that she would use for crusts and cookies.

Memories surfaced of Gram bent over the counter as she meticulously cut designs out of the dough, little leaves or flowers that she would use to decorate the tops of the pies. Pie making was an art for her grandmother, but Gina doubted she would ever have the skill or patience for it. She certainly wouldn't be whipping up a pie for the town meeting.

She wished she didn't have to go to the town meeting; it was pointless because she wasn't staying there. It was a waste of energy to get to know any of the townspeople, and she had little interest in their plan to revitalize Shell Cove. But she couldn't very well refuse to go. Best to just play along.

She was dismayed to discover that a little part of her didn't want to disappoint Maddie. Her cousins were so enthusiastic about the meeting, and Gina could tell Maddie was pinning her hopes on it all working out. Gina didn't wish a disappointment on her, but the odds were about as slim as Gina getting her money back from Hugh.

Her phone pinged, and she picked it up from the counter. An email from Mel keeping her up-to-date with things back home. Back home. But it wasn't really home anymore. She probably wouldn't be able to afford to go back, even though she'd told Mel to look for a condo for her. Everyone thought she was at the beach on vacation and was expecting her to return in a few weeks.

"Are you thinking of making a pie for the meeting?" Maddie's expression was doubtful.

Gina laughed and put the rolling pin down. "No way. I can barely fry an egg. I was just thinking about Gram."

"Yeah, me either. I'm still trying to figure out what to bring." Maddie sat at the table. Her hair was disheveled, and she had a smudge of dust on her nose.

"Where have you been?" Gina asked.

"The storage room. It's over behind the lobby. Turns out there are a lot of things we can use in there—

extra lamps, wall art, even a few bureaus. But the best part is there was a ladder and paint supplies. Now we won't have to buy them and can get started right away." Maddie beamed with excitement, and Gina pretended to be excited too.

"What's all the stuff out on the lawn?" Jules came in from the lobby.

Maddie didn't look up from her computer. "Painting supplies I found in the storage room. I'm making a list of tasks we can start on tomorrow and what we need to buy."

"Oh, right. I guess the sooner we start the better, but maybe we should wait until we find out about the loan?" Jules asked.

"We really only need some paint to start sprucing up the exterior. Paint isn't expensive, so I can spring for that, and we do need to get started," Maddie said.

Ugh… Gina hated the idea of scraping and painting. She wasn't used to manual labor, since she and Hugh always hired it out. But it might be a good opportunity to learn. It didn't appear as if she was going to have the money to hire things out anymore, and she might need those skills. Maybe she could buy a fixer-upper. Perhaps her stint at the Beachcomber would be useful after all.

"I've been thinking about getting started." Jules whipped out her phone, excitement lighting her eyes.

"I've researched some items we need for the rooms to make them more appealing and modern."

She put her phone down on the table and started to scroll through listings of comforters, lamps, and knick-knacks so Maddie could see. Gina's curiosity got the better of her, and she moved closer to look over Maddie's shoulder.

"I was thinking we could paint the furniture we already have white. That always goes nice at the beach. Then we get new comforters and throw pillows and accessories." She scrolled through comforters with beach themes and pillows in beach tones of blues and tans with a pop of color like orange, pink, and turquoise.

Gina started to feel excited. She could already envision how to decorate the rooms. "I don't know if the rooms are all the same, but I think we could move the beds to one wall and paint something behind it... sort of like an artsy headboard. Then maybe pick up some bookshelves at a yard sale and load it with shells and maybe even used books."

"That's a great idea," Maddie said. "People love to read at the beach. It will help make us unique. I was planning on checking out the rest of the rooms today."

"I also think we could bring the theme into the bathrooms. You know, maybe some matching colors and artwork. New shower curtains for sure," Gina suggested.

Jules smiled at Gina over her shoulder. "Great idea."

"Thanks!" Gina beamed. For the first time in a long time, she actually felt useful. Instead of just throwing money at a project and hiring others to do the thinking, she was coming up with ideas on her own. And the look in Jules's eyes said she really thought her idea had value.

Wait… had she and Jules just had a moment of connection? Suddenly cautious, she stepped back. "But we'll have to wait until the loan is approved for all of that."

Jules looked away, her smile faltering. "Of course, I was just getting the research done ahead of time. Speaking of which, we need to research what to bring for the potluck. Pearl called, and it's tomorrow night. I get the impression we can't just buy something at the store. She stressed that people expect the dishes to be homemade."

Gina snorted. "They might be disappointed, then."

"No kidding," Jules said.

Maddie searched on her computer. "Here's a list of easy potluck dishes."

The three of them crowded around and scrolled through.

"Tangy meatballs, cucumber party sandwiches, cilantro tomato bruschetta, fruit kebabs. The kebabs look easy," Maddie said.

"They do, just cut them up and make the dip," Jules agreed.

"I can pick up the fruit and dip ingredients tomorrow," Gina volunteered. Was she getting a little too accommodating? Maybe she shouldn't have offered. But it would give her a chance to get out of the motel and into the town. She could use a break.

"Good. That's settled. Now, let's finish our plan for the painting. I want to get started bright and early tomorrow."

CHAPTER TWELVE

he next morning, Jules was up early and feeling optimistic. She met Maddie in the kitchen. Her cousin was dressed in an old T-shirt and shorts with a pair of Ray-Ban sunglasses perched on top of her head. She was fiddling with the coffee maker.

"Can you start this thing?" Maddie sounded exasperated.

Jules laughed and nudged her away from the machine. "I see you haven't conquered technology yet."

"At least I can work my laptop."

Jules fixed the lid and filled the reservoir. The vintage coffee maker was sort of cute with its perky yellow decor. Maybe she would move it out into the lobby once they were ready for guests. It would be just the sort of thing that would attract interest and get people talking about the motel. Not to mention, it would be handy to make coffee for the guests who wanted to mill about in the lobby or grab a cup to bring out onto the porch.

As she turned to grab the bag of ground coffee, movement in the parking lot caught her eye. She looked out to see Gina's little sports car pulling in a few spots down from her own practical Prius.

"I guess Gina went out shopping already." She watched her cousin take grocery bags out of the car. She looked like she'd just stepped out of a magazine with her oversized sunglasses, silk print shirt, and designer jeans. Why was she even there? Jules doubted she was going to help them with the motel projects, despite the fact that she'd detected a hint of excitement in Gina's tone when they'd discussed the projects last night.

A few seconds later, Gina was in the kitchen balancing three coffees on a takeout tray along with several bags. "I got stuff for the potluck and some other things and... more importantly... coffee for all of us. The stuff that comes out of Mr. Coffee is vile."

She handed a cup to Maddie then one to Jules, careful not to make hand or eye contact. Jules thawed a little. It was nice of Gina to bring back coffees. Opening the tab on the lid, she saw that Gina even remembered that she liked hers with extra milk.

"Thanks." Jules closed the coffee grounds she had

been about to put in the machine and put it in the freezer.

Maddie closed her eyes as she took a sip of hers. "Ahhh. Just what I needed." She put the cup down and rubbed her hands together. "Now are you guys ready to get started? I figure we'll start on the front near the porch and work our way back. We need to keep track of time so we leave ourselves enough time to clean up and make the fruit kebabs for the town meeting."

It was just like Maddie to take over supervision of the plan, but Jules didn't mind. Maddie was a hard worker, too, and it occurred to Jules that they were falling into their old routine they'd had with the Surfstone. Hopefully the venture wouldn't turn out the way that one had.

Jules's stomach roiled at the thought. She simply could not fail at this one. She might never get another chance to prove she could succeed. "I'm ready." Jules took another gulp. Who knew when Maddie would let them have a break?

"Me too." Gina's tone rang with uncertainty, but at least she was agreeing to help out. "The paint is in my trunk."

"Great, then let's get started." Maddie headed toward the door then turned back to Gina. "You might want to change your shirt. I have a feeling things are going to get messy."

CHAPTER THIRTEEN

"These kebabs don't look as good as they did on the website. Maybe we shouldn't bring them in." Maddie stared at the tray in her hand.

It turned out that there was a bit of an art involved with stacking fruit on a stick so that it looked neatly arranged. Theirs looked like it had been through an earthquake.

"We have to. Everyone has something." Jules pointed to a honey-blond with bouncy curls who was walking toward the door with a Crock-Pot. Behind her, an elderly gentleman had a bowl of pasta salad with cut tomatoes artfully arranged on top.

"Right. We don't want to be the only ones."

"Might not matter after what we discovered." Jules's reference to the hole Maddie had made when she'd stepped too hard on the boards on the front porch elicited a sinking feeling.

"Don't worry about that," Maddie said, determined to put up an optimistic front, even though she wasn't quite feeling that way on the inside. "A little rot is to be expected, and we'll be getting funds to fix it soon anyway."

Jules looked skeptical, but then her gaze drifted to something behind Maddie. "The welcome-wagon ladies are here. I suppose we should go in."

Maddie turned to see Rose waving at them from across the parking lot. She was cradling an old-fashioned bowl with blue stripes in her arms. Pearl and Leena were beside her, Pearl with a cake container and Leena with a deviled egg plate similar to the one Maddie remembered from old family cookouts.

"Hi, girls! What did you bring?" Pearl rushed over, her focus on the tray in Maddie's hand, which Maddie wished she could hide.

"Fruit kebabs." Maddie tried to infuse pride into her voice.

Pearl's smile faltered. "Fruit kebabs? Well, I suppose fruit is good for you."

All three of the welcome-wagon ladies were standing there, looking at the plate with various expressions of disappointment. Maddie couldn't blame them.

"Let's go in. I want to get things started." Rose led them toward the meetinghouse. It was an old building, typical of New England meetinghouses, with dozens of layers of white paint, tall windows flanked by green shutters, and a double-door entrance.

Maddie guessed it dated to the mid-eighteen hundreds and still had its original charm. The creaky wooden floorboards were full of scrapes and scars. The ceiling soared twenty feet above them. Metal folding chairs were arranged in neat rows, and a series of folding tables covered in white paper tablecloths were set up in the back. People were congregating around the tables, where one woman was directing the food placement.

Maddie surveyed the food table with its assortment of salads, baked goods, and finger sandwiches all on fancy plates and wrapped in Saran Wrap. She slid the plate next to a tray of chocolates and stood back.

The welcome-wagon ladies introduced Maddie and her cousins to some of the townspeople. Many of them had known Gram, and Maddie appreciated their condolences and kind words about her grandmother. Maddie had a hard time keeping track of all the people. Cassie, the owner of Ocean Brew, which made the fantastic coffee, Deena from Saltwater Sweets, Belinda from the town hall, Lorna, who owned the garden shop.

Maddie noticed Jules wave to a handsome man on the other side of the room.

"Who is that?" Maddie asked.

"Who? That guy?" Jules shrugged. "That's just the guy from the bank. His name is Nick."

"You didn't tell us he was hot," Gina said.

"I didn't notice." Jules feigned indifference, but Maddie could tell from the way she was blushing that she *had* noticed.

Up at the podium, Rose clapped her hands. "Everyone, find a seat. It's time to get started!"

Murmurs of conversation were replaced by the sound of scraping chairs as everyone took their seats.

"First, I'd like to welcome Maddie, Jules, and Gina to town. Most of you have met, I think. They're Rena's granddaughters, and they're going to get the Beachcomber up and running."

Some turned and smiled. Others nodded.

"Won't help. No one comes to town anymore," a man with thick white hair grumped from the back.

Leena twisted around in her front-row seat to address the man. "We're fixing to change that, Dwight. Stop being so negative."

"He does have a point," Deena from Saltwater Sweets piped in. She wasn't nearly as grouchy as Dwight, though, and her soft, sweet voice didn't sound as negative. She looked apologetically at Maddie, Jules, and Gina.

Maddie guessed her to be in her early sixties, though her blond chin-length bob gave her a youthful appearance.

"I don't want you girls to be disappointed," Deena continued.

"Yeah, but tourists *could* come here," Cassie said. "Our town has potential. It's not that far off the main highway, and the scenery is gorgeous."

"Not the main street. That's a dump." The comment came from a purse-lipped woman who Rose had introduced as Constance Harbinger.

Maddie seemed to recall the woman presided over some sort of committee in town. Hopefully she wouldn't ever need her approval for anything to do with the motel.

"It's not exactly a dump. It just needs some sprucing." Rose glared at Constance for a second then smiled again. "Now, here's what we propose."

As Rose listed off ideas on how to spruce up the town, some of the others in the room got excited too. Soon people were making suggestions of their own. The excitement was contagious, and Maddie found herself throwing in a few ideas too. Even though she'd just arrived in town, she felt at home there. Maybe she felt a kinship with the people who were just regular folks with their dreams tied up in the town. She wanted to help them get their dreams back. And maybe she wanted to find a dream of her own.

"It's not just that the town is off the main road," Lorna Baxter said once the conversation died down. "It's that people don't want to drive here because there's not much to see. For the same drive, they can go to Bar Harbor or Old Orchard Beach. We need to give them a reason to come."

"Pffft…" Dwight spouted from the back. "That takes work and planning."

Work and planning? Those were Maddie's specialties. Before she realized what she was doing, she stood up and opened her mouth. "Don't worry about the work or the planning. I think I have an idea. We need an event."

JULES STARED AT MADDIE. HER CHEEKS WERE FLUSHED, and her eyes sparkled with excitement. Did she really have an idea, and had she just volunteered to do all the work and planning?

Dwight spoke, his expression skeptical. "An event? You mean like a fair or something? How would we do that? We're all just hanging on by a thread here."

"Something better than a fair." Maddie tapped her pen on the day planner she was holding open in her lap. "And it won't cost a lot. Maybe a little for advertising."

"I don't know. Why would anyone come there? The place isn't as inviting as it used to be," Constance said.

"It won't take that much to fix it up," Rose said.

"But why bother?" a man leaning against the wall asked.

Leena jumped up from her seat in the front row and turned to address the crowed. "Why bother? Because this is our town, and we love it. Because we've spent our lives here building our businesses. Because we can revive this town and have it back to the way it once was. That's why we should bother."

The room was silent.

Deena cleared her throat. "I think we should at least try."

Cassie nodded. "I agree. What do we have to lose?"

Dwight made a face. "Okay, I guess. I had a lot of respect for Rena, so as long as these girls"—Dwight waved his hand toward Jules, Maddie, and Gina—"are going to do right by the motel, I guess we should give it a shot. A town ain't no good without a motel."

"Okay, it's settled, then. We'll let Maddie come up with a proposal then reconvene."

The words were barely out of Rose's mouth when everyone pushed their chairs back and rushed toward the food table. As they stood in the aisle, waiting for the table to clear, Jules turned to Maddie. "Where did that come from?"

"I have no idea. I just blurted it out." Maddie grimaced, but then her expression turned determined. "But it felt like the right thing, and I'm sure I'll figure out something. The town and the motel need it." Maddie's gaze drifted over Jules's shoulder, and her brows rose. "Looks like someone wants to talk to you."

"What?" Jules turned to see Nick coming toward her.

"Hi." Nick looked good, casual in a T-shirt and jeans, which was a difference from the suit he'd worn at the bank.

"Hi. Maddie and I were just—" Jules turned back only to find empty space where Maddie had been. "Oh well, she was here a minute ago."

Nick laughed. "Guess I scared her off."

"Guess so." Jules smiled, feeling a little awkward. Why had he come over? Maybe he had news about the loan.

"So how do you like our little town so far?" he asked.

"It's great. Needs some work like the motel."

"Sounds like your cousin has a good idea for that."

Jules turned to look for Maddie. She was over at the food table talking to the welcome-wagon ladies and some other townsfolk. "Yeah, she does. We need to attract guests at the motel to pay off the loan that I hope we'll be getting."

Nick looked uneasy for a split second before a coughing sound drew their attention to a man seated in a folding chair against the wall. He was eating a piece of cake and appeared to be ignoring them.

"Is that guy okay?" Jules asked. He seemed okay, but the cough had her worried that he was choking.

Nick turned back to her, taking her arm and

steering her a few steps away from the man. "He's fine. That's my grandfather."

Jules looked over to find the man was staring at her. Hadn't Rose called the man a curmudgeon? "Are you guys close?"

"Yeah." Nick's expression softened. "He practically raised me."

"Does he not like me?" Jules asked.

Nick turned back to look at the old man. "No, he's just grumpy. Don't mind him."

The look on Nick's face made Jules feel sympathetic toward him. He clearly cared for the old curmudgeon, and it reminded Jules of her bond with Gram.

But as they made small talk, Jules got a sinking feeling. Why hadn't Nick mentioned anything about the loan? "We have a call into the lawyer about what we should do for a business structure. How is the loan progressing?"

NICK GLANCED BACK AT HIS GRANDFATHER. WHEN HAD he become such a grump? It had happened gradually, but the Gramps that Nick remembered was always smiling and fun in his childhood. Of course, after his grandmother died, he'd become more somber, but still, instead of growing happier as his grief waned, he'd become more and more grumpy.

Nick turned his attention back to Jules, who was looking up at him, her brown eyes quizzical. Right, she'd asked about the loan, and what was he going to say?

His brain whirred with possibilities. The truth was, he was working an angle with the main bank. Gramps didn't know about it, and he was going to be upset, but Nick knew it was the right thing to do. Gramps's refusal to grant a loan for the Beachcomber Motel was based on emotion, not numbers, and Nick knew he had to try to get that loan, even if it would cause an argument between him and his grandfather.

He glanced up to see Belinda Simms from the town hall leaving, and an idea struck. Before he could think better of it, he blurted, "It's going along fine, but you need to get an occupancy permit for the motel before we can go any further."

Jules's brow creased. "A permit? I've never heard of that as criteria for a loan."

"We need to make sure that it can be occupied so you can get guests and start an income to pay back the loan." Nick's cheeks burned. He wasn't a very good liar, and now that he thought about it, that was one of the dumbest things he'd ever said. What had he been thinking?

"Oh, okay. I guess I can do that. I think I met the town hall lady here."

"She just left." Nick's gut churned. What was going

to happen when Jules went to the town hall? They would need a permit for the motel eventually. He could talk to Ryan and tell him the bank wanted a pre-inspection or something. Maybe that would just be a way for them to get an occupancy permit sooner. Maybe he'd just helped her out?

"Okay. I guess I'll go down there first thing tomorrow, then," Jules said, her voice optimistic.

"Yeah. Good idea."

"So everything is going okay, then?"

"Yep. Going along good." Nick searched for something to change the conversation with. "I uhh… I'm working on those business accounts for you."

"Okay, great," Jules said. They stared at each other for a few awkward beats, then she added, "So I guess I'll see you around then."

Jules started to back away, and Nick almost reached out to grab her arm so she would stay, but his brain wasn't working right. All he could really think about was rushing back to the bank and making sure he could get that loan to go through before Jules discovered that he'd just told her a whopper of a lie.

HENRY FORKED UP ANOTHER PIECE OF CAKE. THE CAKE part was delicious, but the frosting was too sweet. Pearl had always put too much sugar in her frosting when they were younger, and it looked like things hadn't changed much. He glanced over at his grandson and the Whittier girl, a faint longing tugging at his heart. She looked just like her grandmother. The same chocolate curls, the same brown eyes. And he remembered looking into those eyes, which had seemed so sincere... until she left town without a word.

His heart hardened as he watched the two talk. Nick had that goofy look on his face, and Henry resisted the urge to warn him. There was nothing Henry could do about it. He knew he would have to let it play its course.

After his wife died, he never thought he would feel that way about anyone again. But then his friendship with Rena had turned into something more. At least he'd thought it had, and he was sure she felt the same way too. But apparently not, judging by her actions.

Too bad Nick had taken the girl out of earshot when she'd asked about the loan. Was Nick still trying to give the Beachcomber a loan? If so, part of him was angry about Nick going against his wishes, but the other part glowed with pride. Nick going against him and standing up for something was what he'd wished for his grandson for a long time. He just wished it wasn't on this particular subject.

He felt guilty about shutting Nick down over the loan, but he'd been angry. The way Rena had left town with no explanation had given him a bad taste in his mouth about women in general, and Whittiers in particular. Besides, it was probably a bad investment. Although, from what he'd heard at the town meeting tonight, maybe there was hope for the town and the Beachcomber Motel after all. But deep down, he knew you couldn't trust women.

He bet his grandson hadn't told Jules that the bank wouldn't approve the loan. She wouldn't be smiling up at him like that if he had.

He wondered what Nick was telling her. Come to think of it, he had been acting a little secretive at the bank. Was Nick up to something? If so, Henry might have to pretend to be angry, but it wouldn't last long. Because when it came down to it, he loved Nick more than anything, and he wasn't going to let something like a silly loan put a rift in their relationship.

GINA STOOD AT THE FOOD TABLE, PLATE IN HAND. HER gaze drifted over the bowls of salads, trays of appetizers, and plates of desserts. She'd never seen so much home-cooked food in one place. And the people seemed so proud of their creations, many of them oohing and aahing over each other's dishes and exchanging tips and recipes.

She'd never really cooked when she was younger, and once she married Hugh, they'd had a personal chef. She got the impression she'd missed out, though. The proud expressions on people's faces indicated that it was very satisfying to come up with a good dish.

Her gaze fell on the fruit kebabs she'd made with her cousins. They really did pale in comparison to the other offerings. Hugh's hurtful words about her not having any skills ran through her mind. He wasn't wrong. She couldn't even cut fruit properly. But she could scrape paint off a house pretty well. At least she'd discovered that during their renovation.

"Those are some nice wheels you got there." Rose came to stand beside her and picked a brownie off the tray. "I used to have one like that when I was young."

They'd taken Gina's Mazda to the town meeting, and the little red sports car was sitting in the parking lot, looking out of place among the Oldsmobiles and Toyotas. She did love that car, but unfortunately, she would have to sell it soon because her latest payments were past due. Maybe she could trade it in at the used-car lot in town for something much cheaper and walk away with a bit of cash.

"It's a little much. I'm thinking of trading it in for something more practical now that we're renovating the motel and everything," she said to Rose, just so no one would think she had to sell it.

Rose nodded as she munched on her brownie. "How's the renovation going?"

"Well, it's funny you ask. We're doing okay with the painting and scraping, but we discovered some rotted wood that made a big hole in the porch, and that's a little bit beyond our skill set."

"Oh, really? It just so happens my grandson is a very good carpenter. I could talk to him and see if he could take a look at it," Rose said.

Gina frowned. "I don't know. We don't have any money to pay him."

Rose's gaze drifted to Jules and Nick, who were deep in conversation. "Well, it looks like you might be getting that loan soon. Besides, I'm sure Dex would be happy to defer payment."

"Really?" Gina asked.

"Sure. He does it all the time for the townspeople, and this job is important."

"That sounds like an option. I'll talk to my cousins and see if they agree. When could he start?"

Rose looked quite pleased with the idea of Dex working at the motel. "I'm pretty sure he could start right away."

CHAPTER FOURTEEN

*G*ina woke early the next morning to an email with another past-due bill for her car payment. She'd dreamt all night about making pies with her grandmother. She felt warm and comfortable cocooned in memories of rolling out the dough, making the filling, and adding the finishing touches. Not that she could do it on her own. She didn't even know what ingredients to use.

Jules and Maddie were still asleep, so she made coffee and got settled in one of the wicker rockers on the front porch, carefully avoiding the big hole in the middle. The sun was shining. The birds were chirping. The coffee was adequate, though she much preferred the brew from the cafe in town. But sitting there on the porch, with the sun on her face and the waves crashing on the shore just below her, it felt like heaven.

The landscaping needed work, she thought as she sat rocking and sipping her coffee. Maybe some flowers in front, a few shrubs over by the stairs, and some bird feeders would really spruce the place up. People loved watching birds, and they would add a lively show. But she wasn't going to be there that long. Eventually, someone would find Hugh, and she would get her money back. Wouldn't she?

Except right then, it was the best place for her. It was free to stay, and her money was running out. She glanced at her car in the parking lot and wondered again how much she could get for it. Did used-car lots let people trade in a car worth more than the one they were buying?

She pulled out her phone to search but found herself looking at pies instead. She remembered yesterday when Jules had looked up recipes for the town meeting. Maybe she should look up recipes for pies.

The side door squeaked open, and Maddie came out. Gina put her phone facedown in her lap so Maddie couldn't see what she'd been searching.

"Thanks for making the coffee." Maddie slipped into the other rocker with her mug.

"You're welcome. I wanted to go to the cafe, but I figured we wouldn't have time. We should start working as soon as possible." Gina stretched. Her muscles were a little sore, but it felt good to do real work.

Beside her, Maddie rocked silently, which was

unusual because she was always chipperly chattering about something.

"Is something wrong?" Gina asked.

"Well, it's just that I blurted out that bit about having an event in town that would bring people, and I really have no ideas on what that would be." Maddie sipped her coffee and shrugged. "So I guess the pressure is on."

Gina thought it would help to have an event that would bring people to town, but she didn't have any clue as to what that might be. She probably wouldn't even be there by then.

"Jules is going to see about that permit today, but we can start working without her." Maddie's gaze drifted to the hole in the porch, and she frowned. "And then there's this hole in the porch. I hope that won't hinder this occupancy permit that Jules is supposed to get for the loan."

Gina felt a bit alarmed. Would it? That could ruin all their plans, but then, did she really care? "Rose mentioned her grandson might do the work."

"She mentioned him to me too. But I wonder how good he is if he's available to start right away."

"There probably isn't much work in this town, and maybe this is the slow season."

"If there's not a lot of work, then why does he stay?" Maddie asked.

"Family, maybe? At least we could try him out. We

don't have a long time to wait on this. And Rose did say he'd defer payment, which we need because we don't know when the loan will come in."

Maddie sighed and looked resigned. "I guess you're right. Let's talk to Jules when she gets back, and we'll see if we can get him to come give us an estimate."

Jules decided to stop in at Ocean Brew on the way home from the town hall. Applying for the occupancy permit had gone smoother than she'd thought. The only catch was that Belinda had said they needed to have the motel inspected. That was a little worrisome, considering the condition, but Jules had assumed they would take that into consideration.

Cassie greeted her with a welcoming smile. That was the thing about small towns. Everyone was always so nice. Or at least they seemed that way.

"Jules, right?" Cassie asked as she approached the counter.

"That's right. Nice to see you again."

"You too. What can I get you?"

Jules knew her cousins liked lattes, so she ordered three of them. Cassie chatted with her as she got busy making them.

"So, how are things at the motel?"

"Good. I just got an occupancy permit."

Cassie frowned. "Oh, is it ready for guests? I thought it needed work."

"It does, but we need the permit to get the loan."

Cassie's frown deepened. She looked like she was about to say something, but then her gaze shifted to the customer who had just come in behind Jules. "Speaking of loans…"

Jules turned to see Nick. "Oh, hi. We meet again." Jules blurted out the first thing that came to mind.

Nick shrugged. "Everyone meets at Ocean Brew sooner or later. Can I buy you a coffee?" He gestured toward the little booth next to the window, as if inviting her to sit.

Jules didn't really know how to respond. She had to get back to the motel, but it wouldn't hurt to butter up the guy who was going to give them a loan.

"I was getting lattes for my cousins," she said.

"I could hold off on those, and you guys can chat. I'll make them fresh when you're done." Cassie shoved Jules's latte across the counter then looked at Nick. "Black coffee for you, Nick?"

"Yep. I'll pay for all of these."

"Okay. Well, thanks." Jules went to the booth, and Nick joined her a few seconds later.

"I just came from the town hall getting the occupancy permit for the loan," Jules said.

"Oh." Nick's gaze fell to his coffee, and Jules got an uneasy feeling.

Did he know something about the permit or the inspection? News traveled fast in a small town, but if he did, he didn't mention it.

"That's great. Things are rolling along at the bank. Sorry to make you wait."

"No problem. I hear your grandfather still goes into work every day. Is he okay after last night?" Jules asked.

"He's fine. He just can be a little grumpy at times." Nick took a sip of his coffee.

"My Gram was like that. It's really special when you have a relationship with them."

Nick's warm smile made her heart flutter. "It really is. You must have been close with yours. She left you a motel, and your cousins too."

"We were close," Jules said. At least she was with her grandmother. Her cousins, not so much. "And even though the motel needs a lot of work, she wanted me to revive it." Jules glanced out the window at the dilapidated town. "I don't want to disappoint her, but it's a big job, and the town, well…"

Nick followed her gaze. "Yeah, I know the town isn't exactly in its heyday, but your cousin sounded like she had some ideas. Maybe it won't be so hard to bring people back here."

Jules sipped her coffee. "Let's hope. I made Gram a promise, and I don't want to disappoint her."

Nick nodded. "I know what you mean. I hate to

disappoint my grandfather too. I promised I'd help keep the bank afloat."

Jules felt a sympathetic connection with Nick. She knew how it was to try to keep promises, even if things were working against them. "It must be hard with the town the way it is."

"You can say that again, but let's hope better days are coming." Nick raised his coffee cup, and they clinked rims.

"Let's hope," she said.

Nick looked out over the town, and Jules took a moment to study him. He had a handsome face, a strong jaw. Sitting near the window with the sun shining in made his eyes more of an amber than brown. But why was she noticing things like that? She was not in the market for a boyfriend. The last one hadn't worked out so well.

Suddenly feeling awkward, she grasped at the first thing she could to make small talk. "So, did you grow up here in town?"

Nick's attention turned back to the table. "Yes, I did. Born and raised."

"It's a beautiful place," she said. "There's not a lot going on, but that's part of its charm, I think."

Nick took a sip of his coffee. "What about you?"

"I grew up in a small beach town, too, near Lobster Bay, just down the coast of Maine."

"I've been there. It's very nice."

Jules nodded. "It's a lot like here."

"It is," Nick said. "So, will you be staying here after you get the motel up and running?"

Jules thought about that. Part of her vision of being successful was that she would run the motel, just like Gram had run all of hers. Well, except for the one that Jules and her cousins had ruined. The town was growing on her, and the people seemed nice. Especially Nick. He was worth getting to know better as a friend.

His phone chirped, and he pulled it out of his pocket. "Oh, I've got a meeting in five. Better get back to the bank. Nice talking to you. It's good to know the newcomers better." He got up from the table.

"You too," Jules said as she watched him leave.

She liked Nick, maybe more than she should, but her focus was on the motel. Even so, things were looking up here. Even Gina seemed to be coming around.

"THOSE TWO LOOKED COZY," LEENA SAID AS SHE watched Nick leave the coffee shop.

She, Pearl, and Rose had pulled up in front of Ocean Brew and spied Jules and Nick in the booth.

"I think they make a cute couple," Rose said.

"Hopefully he's not as sour as his grandfather," Pearl piped in.

"No kidding. I don't know though. He hasn't found a girl that sticks yet. I don't think he's the type that makes a commitment." Leena had known Nick since he was a baby. In a small town, everyone knew who everyone dated and for how long.

"I think you're wrong, Lee. He's a sweet guy. Remember when he saved that duck that got stuck in the ice at Pine Pond?" Pearl asked.

"That was really sweet of him." Leena smiled at the memory. "He took a big risk, and he could have fallen in, but that's different from romance. I think Henry has turned him off of that."

Rose twisted in her seat to look at Leena in the back. "I think Jules might change his mind. Have you seen the way he looks at her?"

"Well, there's only one thing to do in this situation," Pearl said. "We need a wager."

"Great idea. I'll put five on the romance," Rose said.

Leena whipped a five-dollar bill out of her wallet and handed it to Rose. "And I'll put five on no romance."

Pearl dug in her coat pocket and produced a crumpled bill. "I'm going for the romance too." She handed it to Rose.

Rose shoved the bills into the little compartment in her console, unclipped her seat belt, and opened the door. She turned to look at the other two women. "Are you guys coming? I need a cappuccino to get me going."

Jules was just exiting the coffee shop with three to-go cups in hand as they got to the door. She smiled when she saw them. "Hey, how are you today?"

"Just dandy, and you? I noticed you with Nick Barlowe." Rose nodded toward the booth they'd been sitting in.

Jules blushed, and Pearl shot Leena a smug look. Leena wasn't worried. She was actually rooting for Jules and Nick to get together. The boy needed to be reminded that having someone in his life was a good thing. Henry's attitude was starting to poison him, but she didn't want to admit that. She had to keep up her gruff reputation.

"We ran into each other here," Jules said. "It doesn't hurt to be nice to the person who is handing out loans."

The ladies nodded.

"So how is the loan going?" Rose asked.

"Good, I applied for the occupancy permit just this morning."

The three ladies exchanged glances.

"So soon?" Leena asked.

Jules nodded. "I need it for the loan."

"You don't say. That seems odd," Rose said.

Jules shrugged. "I thought so, too, but that's what Nick said."

"I've never applied for a loan for a motel, so I guess I don't know the procedure," Rose said.

"Hopefully the inspection will be okay. We do need some work done there."

Rose nodded. "Yes, I suggested my grandson to Gina the other night."

"She told me. We're going to call him for an estimate."

"That's good. He'll do a good job for you."

"I'm sure he will. Well, I better get going." Jules held up the coffees. "Don't want these to get cold."

"Of course not. Has Maddie mentioned anything more about her idea?" Rose asked as Jules turned to leave.

Jules frowned. "No, but she's working on it."

"I know she'll come up with something great," Pearl said.

They watched Jules exit.

"That is odd about the permit. I wonder what Nick is up to." Leena shot a smug look at Pearl. "Maybe he is playing some games with our little friend."

"Nick's not really a game player, but it does seem curious," Pearl said.

"The usual, ladies?" Cassie asked from behind the counter.

"Yes, please," all three answered.

Rose's phone pinged as they made their way up to

the counter, and she rummaged in her purse. "It's from Dex. He can start on the motel tomorrow."

"But the girls haven't even agreed," Leena said.

"Don't worry. They will." Rose sounded sure of herself.

Pearl tutted and shook her head. "Well, that ought to be interesting. Three pretty girls and that charmer grandson of yours. What could go wrong?"

CHAPTER FIFTEEN

*M*addie practically jumped off the ladder when Jules showed up with coffee from Ocean Brew.

"Thanks so much. How did things go at the town hall?" She accepted the Styrofoam cup from her cousin.

"I filled out the permit application, but we need an inspection." Jules's eyes fell to the big hole in the porch. "She said the inspector might come tomorrow."

"We do? But we're still renovating." Maddie wondered about the outcome of the inspection. What if they failed?

"I guess they take that into consideration. Rose said something about her grandson coming to fix the porch, anyway."

"Yeah," Gina piped in, the first thing she'd said

since Jules came back, and she silently accepted the coffee.

While the cousins weren't arguing anymore, they weren't exactly buddies either. Maddie would have to work harder on that.

"Rose mentioned him to me. We were just discussing him earlier and thought we'd wait for you to get back so we could discuss it."

Maddie's gaze was pulled toward the ocean. It had been calling her all day with the gentle breeze and the cadence of the waves, the seagulls cawing up above. She was dying to dig her toes into the fine white sand on the beach. "How about we enjoy our coffees on the beach while we talk?"

"Great idea." Jules was the first to reach the steps, and Maddie and Gina followed her down.

Maddie sat on one of the large rocks and dug her toes into the warm sand while Jules sat on a piece of sun-bleached driftwood that had washed up long ago.

"So, what do you know about this Dex?" Jules asked Gina.

Gina shrugged. "Rose didn't say much about him. Really, just he's good and available."

"Of course she would say he's good. It's her grandson." Maddie was still skeptical about the guy. Being so organized herself, she couldn't imagine someone who was any good having an opening for work. Maybe he wasn't very ambitious, which might not bode well toward getting the project done in a timely manner.

"Maybe we should get a few quotes," Jules suggested, apparently sensing Maddie's hesitation.

Maddie sighed. Her earlier Google search for local carpenters had not met with success. "The closest one is at least an hour away."

"Who will want to drive an hour for a small job like that hole?" Gina had remained standing, probably so she wouldn't have to sit next to Jules.

Maddie had racked her brain for ways to get them to ease into being friends again. She felt sure if they just worked on a project side by side, the ice would crack. But what project?

"I guess we don't have much choice, then. If someone has to drive an hour to get here, that's going to increase the costs dramatically. Maybe we should try this Dex guy out," Jules said.

"I suppose you're right." Maddie set aside her misgivings and returned to her usual optimistic self. "We're going to need to get that porch fixed quickly, and soon we'll be starting on the inside. I think I should order those items you found, Jules."

Jules looked excited. "Really? But what about the money?"

"I have a little in savings that I could contribute." Maddie glanced at Gina. Surely she had a ton of money and wouldn't miss a few thousand if she invested it in the motel. But Gina remained silent, gazing out into the ocean as if she were oblivious to their financial situation.

Maddie turned to Jules and caught her watching Gina with a look of disgust. Jules had been wondering the same thing about Gina pitching in. Ugh. Maddie hoped that wouldn't drive them further apart.

"I have some savings, too, I can pitch in," Jules said. "Maybe we can pay ourselves back when we get the loan."

"Another reason to hire Rose's grandson. He'll defer payment," Gina said.

"Right. I'll let Rose know." Jules had put the three ladies' contact information into her phone earlier. She pulled it out and messaged Rose.

"Thanks," Maddie said.

"But eventually we'll have to pay him." Jules turned to Maddie. "So, what was your big idea to bring people to town that you were so excited about at the town meeting?"

Maddie's spirits fell like a lead balloon. "That's a bit of a problem. I don't actually have an idea, yet, but I'm working on it."

Jules patted her knee. "Don't worry. I'm sure you'll think of something."

Maddie was heartened by her cousin's support. At first, she'd been afraid that their prior venture into motel running would make Jules not want to work with her, but she seemed to have let bygones be bygones, at least when it came to Maddie.

"Even when you do figure something out, it might not work. Not everyone seemed on board with fixing up the town," Gina said.

"Some are skeptical, but I think we can change their minds." Maddie refused to become pessimistic.

Jules's phone dinged, and she looked at it. "That was Rose. Dex can start tomorrow if we want." She looked up at her cousins questioningly.

Gina nodded. "Sure. Why not?"

Maddie shrugged, her optimism winning out over her caution. "Tell her to send him over first thing. What have we got to lose?"

CHAPTER SIXTEEN

Gina walked along the row of cars in the used-car lot and realized she had no idea what to look for in a car. Was she supposed to open the hood and check the engine? She just wanted one that was dependable and was at least somewhat as nice as what she was used to.

"Hello there. Can I help you?" A smiling woman in a black pantsuit was coming toward her from the door of the building.

Gina sighed. Hopefully she could talk her into taking her car and giving her some cash in return. "Hi." Gina pasted a friendly smile on her face. "I was thinking about trading in my car for something less... flashy."

The woman glanced back at the red Miata. "Nice car. I don't know if we have anything up to that standard."

"Oh, I don't want anything flashy like that. I'd really just like something more practical."

The woman gave her a quizzical look, as if puzzling out why someone would downgrade their car.

Gina leaned toward her, her expression serious. "Divorce."

"Oh!" The woman's right hand went to her left ring finger. She didn't wear a ring, but Gina guessed she'd been divorced herself, judging by her reaction. "I totally understand. I'm Sheila Landry. You must be one of the women working on the Beachcomber."

Gina stuck out her hand. "Gina Gallagher. Pleased to meet you."

"Likewise. How are things going at the motel?" Sheila glanced out over the lot. "Uncle Bernie was at the town meeting, and he was excited about the changes in town. If we could get the people back…" She sighed and looked out over the lot. "Well, it would be good for all of us."

"It sure would." Gina hadn't given much thought to the fact that an influx of tourists would benefit the other businesses in town. She'd mostly just been thinking about how it would help the Beachcomber, but she could see it was bigger than that. For the first time in a long time, she felt proud and hopeful to be a part of something that might impact others in a positive way.

"Anything here catch your eye?" Sheila gestured toward the rows of cars.

"I kind of like this blue one." Gina didn't even know what kind of car it was, but she liked the color, and the interior looked comfortable.

"That's a Honda Accord, a really good car. It gets good mileage and is reliable." Sheila spouted off some of the features of the car as she led Gina toward it. "It's only two years old. It's a really good buy."

"Would you take my car as a trade-in?" Gina knew her car was worth almost ten thousand more than the price tag on the Honda. She still owed a couple thousand on the loan, but maybe she could walk away with some money in her pocket.

Sheila glanced back at the Mazda and pressed her lips together. "Generally, we don't take trades that are worth more than the sale." She looked back at Gina, her face softening. "But if you take this one for a test drive and still want to buy it, maybe we could work something out."

"Sounds good. Let's go for a ride."

Two hours later, Gina drove off with the Honda and a check for ten thousand in her pocket. It turned out that Sheila had had a similar experience as Gina during her divorce. Who knew bonding over divorce would help her get what she wanted?

The Honda had been ready to go, and they'd been able to do the paperwork quickly since she wasn't applying for financing. She'd transferred a few things from her car, then she was off to get the new one registered.

As she sat in the Honda familiarizing herself with the controls, she remembered her cousins talking about how they would contribute from their savings in order to buy the things they needed for the motel rooms. She'd felt guilty not pitching in, but the truth was she had no money, and besides, she wasn't really that invested in the outcome of the motel. Still, it was only right that she pitch in, even if she didn't plan to stay out the project. Hugh always said to use other people's money, but he ripped people off, including her. She wasn't on board with that anymore.

She sighed and mentally allocated two thousand dollars from what she'd received. It wasn't really lost money. Jules had said they would pay themselves back when they got the loan.

She put the paperwork on the passenger seat, jostling her phone, which lit up, displaying the pie recipes she'd looked up online. The ingredients were pretty simple: flour, sugar, butter. Maybe she should pick some up at the market and try a recipe.

As she drove off, she felt uneasy. Contributing money to the motel project and baking pies? What was happening to her?

MADDIE SAT IN THE KITCHEN OF THE MOTEL AND looked down at the blank piece of paper. She was supposed to be making a list of events that could bring people to the town, but so far, no good ideas had materialized.

A car pulled in, and she looked out the window. It was a blue Honda she didn't recognize.

"Who's that?" Jules turned from her place at the sink, where she'd been washing out the paintbrushes.

Gina got out with several bags of groceries. "It's Gina. But whose car does she have? Looks like she brought some food. I hope she got peanut butter."

Gina came to the side door that led straight to the kitchen, and Maddie opened the door for her.

"Hey, guys. I stocked up."

"Did you get peanut butter and bread?" Maddie asked.

Gina nodded. "And Fluff."

"What's with the car?" Jules asked as Gina started to put the groceries away.

Gina shrugged, her back to them. "It reminded me of my ex, so I got rid of it. It was fun, but I felt like something more practical was better for me now. I liked the color of this one."

Maddie wondered about that. The new car was

quite a step down from her sports car, and while it could be true that Gina didn't want to be reminded of Hugh, Maddie had a hard time believing that she wouldn't spring for a more luxurious model.

Gina pulled a stack of bills out of her pocket and put them on the table. "I wanted to contribute to buying the comforters and decorations for the motel rooms. I would've said something earlier, but all my money is tied up because of the divorce."

"Thanks." Maddie neatened the bills into an even pile, glancing up to see that Gina was unloading things like flour and sugar. "Hey, that looks like baking goods. Are you going to bake something?"

Gina shrugged. "Well, if you come up with an idea for the town, we'll have another town meeting, right?"

"I suppose so," Maddie said.

"And the welcome-wagon ladies will want signature dishes," Gina said. "Last time it was a little embarrassing with those fruit kebabs."

"You do have a point," Jules said. "But are you going to make a pie? I think those are hard."

"Maybe." Gina went back to putting things away. "Gram taught me how to make dough, but that was a really long time ago. I thought it would be nice to try, though, since it was her specialty. I don't know how to do anything else, anyway."

"I think that will be great," Maddie said to encourage her cousin. Plus, she liked to eat pie.

"So, what have you come up with for ideas?" Jules looked at the blank piece of paper on the table.

"Pretty much nothing." Maddie felt exasperated. "I've had a few, but some are too complicated. Others would take too much money. We need something that will attract a lot of people, but judging by the reaction in the town hall, no one is going to fork over a lot of money to set it up or advertise it."

Gina turned from the cabinet where she was putting the flour away. "What about a contest or something that people can win a prize?"

Maddie didn't want to discourage Gina. That was the first time she'd seemed to want to get involved, but where would they get the prize money? "That could attract a lot of people, but what kind of contest, and how much would we need to set up for it?"

"Maybe a fishing contest. People fish for stripers off the pier, and there's that empty donut shop. Maybe we could use it for something," Jules offered. "Word of mouth would get around with the fishermen, and we might not have to spend so much on advertising."

Maddie sat back and thought about it. She didn't know the first thing about a fishing contest, and they would still need a substantial amount for the prize money in order to draw enough people. And would it even be the right kind of people? They needed tourists, people who would spend time in the town then tell their friends how great it was. She didn't think fishermen fit the bill. But something Jules had said struck a chord. If she could figure out something that people would come to see and that basically advertised for itself, that might make it cheaper. But what?

CHAPTER SEVENTEEN

"I'm handling this loan a little differently."
Nick glanced out of his office to make sure his grandfather wasn't around. Nick was on the phone with the regional vice president, Gary Sunderland, about the Beachcomber Motel loan.

"That's good. It's time your grandfather delegated more responsibility." Gary had actually been after Henry to retire. Most bank managers did that well before Henry's age, but he'd done such a good job at the bank, and no one really wanted to fill his role, so they let him stay on since he still wanted to.

"You can say that again." Nick did wish his grandfather would at least slow down a little and focus on enjoying life more.

"Why don't you fax the loan application and credit checks over, and I'll take a look?" Gary asked. "It's a bit of a special case, but if the motel is that important to the town, maybe we can work something out."

Nick breathed a sigh of relief. "Okay, great. Thanks."

"No problem."

"Oh, and, Gary. I'd appreciate it if you didn't mention this to Gramps. He's got a heavy workload, and you know how he tries to take things on himself."

"No problem. Mum's the word."

Nick hung up, feeling guilty about going behind Gramps's back but also happy that the loan had a chance, even though he'd told Gary the credit reports hadn't exactly been stellar.

"Did I hear you talking to Gary?" Gramps appeared in the doorway.

"Oh, no. I mean, yeah. Just discussing the new deposit process." His guilt deepened. It wasn't totally a lie. The bank did have a new process for deposits, and Nick's conversation with Gary had included that.

Gramps looked concerned. "Is something wrong?"

"No. Nope. Everything is just fine." Nick forced a smile, even though everything really wasn't fine. He'd gone behind Gramps's back, and that was not going to go over well. But even worse, he'd told that stupid lie about the Beachcomber needing an occupancy permit. Why had he done that? If Jules dug deeper into that, she might find out the truth.

Hopefully his causal conversation with Belinda at

the town hall had kept her from being suspicious of Jules's request for a permit. Another little lie to add to his guilt, he'd told Belinda that occupancy permits for commercial businesses might become part of the loan process.

But what if Ryan went to inspect the place and it didn't pass? Nick wouldn't go so far as to ask Ryan to fake the report. He would have to hope the motel was in good enough condition. If it did fail, they could get it inspected again.

Gramps shuffled away, and Nick stared at his screen blankly. The only thing that could save him was if the loan came through before his lie was discovered.

CHAPTER EIGHTEEN

The next morning, Maddie was painting the trim on the side of the motel with Gina and Jules when a rusty pickup truck pulled into the parking lot.

"That must be Rose's grandson." Gina paused to watch him, paint dripping from her brush. She was dressed in a T-shirt and shorts, paint already splattered on the front. At least she'd found something other than the designer silk shirts she had been wearing. Maddie would have hated to see those ruined.

Maddie had been concentrating so much on the painting that she'd lost track of time. She quickly descended the ladder, balanced her brush on top of the open can of paint, and wiped her hands on the paint cloth as she waited for the man to get out of the truck.

The door of the truck squealed open, and several

coffee-stained Styrofoam cups fell out, followed by a stack of receipts. A tall, lanky guy stepped out.

"He's kind of cute," Jules whispered.

"Cute?" Maddie watched as he bent to pick up the trash that had spilled out of his car and shove it back inside. "He seems like a disaster."

He turned to face them and smiled. He was kind of cute, though she wasn't a fan of the five o'clock shadow or the way his sun-kissed hair curled down below his ears. But he did have a nice smile, the kind that could convince a girl to make bad decisions. That made Maddie even more distrusting of him.

"Hi. I'm Dex Wheeler."

A round of introductions ensued, and Dex's charming demeanor even garnered a smile from Gina.

"Why don't you show me what you need?" he asked. They went to the porch, and he knelt down to inspect the hole. "Wood rot. You might have carpenter ants too."

"Great." Maddie mentally pictured their loan money circling a drain in their bank account.

"Nothing that can't be fixed." Dex stood, his earnest green eyes assessing them. "I can start right away if you'd like."

Maddie remembered Jules mentioning that the inspector for the occupancy permit might come that day. Could Dex repair it before he came? If not, she supposed it would be in their best interest to show they were having it repaired. Normally she would want to get three estimates from different contractors before she hired anyone, but this guy was the only one available, so there was no need to not let him start immediately. She glanced at Gina and Jules, who both nodded. "Sounds good. Do you need anything? What about wood to replace the rotted parts?"

"I'll buy the wood and put it on the bill. I recommend pressure treated, and you should consider replacing the entire porch eventually, but I can fix just the parts that need it now if money is tight. I get a discount, so that will actually save you some money. I've set my billing software to make the due date ninety days out. And if you need more work, I'm available for the summer."

He had software? She'd pictured him scribbling the bill out on a stained napkin. Maybe he wasn't as disorganized and unprofessional as he appeared. And his willingness to defer the payment did soften her attitude toward him a little.

"Okay, that would be great if you could start now. The porch fix is all we need, though."

His gaze flicked over the motel, and he frowned. "If you say so."

Maddie felt her patience slipping. "We only want the porch fixed."

"We're waiting on a bank loan," Jules cut in. "So we

don't want to rack up too much of a bill before we find out about that."

"Yeah, I heard. Don't worry. Nick will make it happen. I don't need the money right now. Besides, it's a favor for Gram. So if you need other work done…" He looked over the motel again as if any idiot could see they would. "I'm your guy."

Maddie crossed her arms over her chest. "So, how much will it be to fix the porch? Are you going to write up an estimate?"

"Sure. I can do that, but I'm the only carpenter in the area, so you're kind of stuck with me."

Maddie bristled at his arrogance. "I think it would be prudent."

"Okay." He drew out the word as if placating a child as he pulled a stained piece of paper out of his back pocket. He slid a pencil out from behind his ear and started scribbling. After a minute or so, he handed it over. "Here you go."

Maddie stared at it in disbelief. "Five hundred bucks? That seems cheap."

He shrugged. "You're friends with Gram, so I gave you the friends and family discount."

Gina grabbed the piece of paper before Maddie could complain further. "Looks good. You're hired."

Maddie leveled a look at her and glanced at Jules. Something didn't ring true about his cheap price. No one was that nice. Was it some kind of bait and switch? She might be overly optimistic and positive about things, but when it came to business, she didn't like to be taken advantage of, even though in his case, it was more like them taking advantage of him.

Jules lifted her left brow. "I agree. That's pretty cheap for this work. You know what Gram always said about looking a gift horse in the mouth."

"You might get bit?" Dex asked.

Maddie looked at him incredulously. That was exactly what Gram had always said. "How did you know?"

He laughed. "My gram always says that too."

A car pulled into the parking lot.

"Who's that?" Gina asked.

Dex looked perplexed. "That's Ryan Connelly, the building inspector. Did you apply to have my work inspected already? Even I don't work that fast."

"No," Maddie said. "Maybe he's here for the occupancy permit?"

"Occupancy?" Dex looked at the hole in the porch again. "It might be a little premature to start having guests here."

"It's not for that. It's for the loan," Jules said.

"Huh?" Dex looked at her. "Why would you need an inspection for a loan?"

Jules's smile faltered. "Nick said it was a contingency on the loan approval."

"Hey, Dex." A short, stocky man in a blue button-down shirt and tan chinos approached.

"Hey, Ryan, this is Maddie, Jules, and Gina," Dex introduced them. "Jules was telling me this inspection is for the loan. When did you start doing that?"

Ryan looked confused. "This isn't for any loan that I know of. That wouldn't make sense, especially if the loan is for repairs. The inspection needs to be done after the repairs."

Maddie glanced at Jules, whose look of confusion was quickly turning to anger.

"Wait. You mean this isn't something to make sure the motel will eventually be habitable?" Jules asked.

"Umm, no, this is the real thing." Ryan tapped his clipboard, his expression indicating that he was doubtful the motel would pass.

"Wait," Maddie said. "So we're going to fail, then?"

"Hold on!" Dex put up his hands. "I think there has been a misunderstanding. We don't want the inspection to fail, but what if I take you around and show you the intended repairs? Then you can get a head start on it and come back later for the final approval once they are done. That might be good enough for the bank."

Ryan shrugged. "Okay, I guess that could work."

Dex led him off, turning back to wink at them as he rounded the corner.

"Wow. I think he just saved the day," Gina said. "Maybe you misunderstood them at the bank, Jules."

"No, I don't think I did. But I'm going to go down there right now and find out why I was misled."

Maddie and Gina watched Jules storm off.

"Uh-oh, sounds like this could be trouble," Gina said. "I hope she doesn't piss off the bank guy. We may not get that loan at all."

"Me too." Maddie didn't like the way it was going. Now, more than ever, she needed to come up with an event that would bring people to town.

And for that, she needed decent coffee.

CHAPTER NINETEEN

*J*ules stormed through the lobby of the bank, barely acknowledging the greeting of the smiling teller. She turned down the hall where the offices were and stopped in front of Nick's.

His desk faced the door, so she could see the look of surprise and something else—was that guilt?—on his face when he looked up.

He jumped up. "Jules. Hi. I was just working on your loan."

"Really? That's why I'm here. The inspector is at the motel right now. Funny thing though. He seemed confused about the inspection being a criterion for the loan."

Nick looked uncomfortable. "Err... well... that's a bank thing and not anything to—"

She cut him off. "The inspection isn't required for the loan, is it?"

"Well, I guess not technically, but you need an inspection, and we do need to know if you'll be able to generate an income."

"Did you lie about the inspection?" Jules demanded.

Nick looked like a child who had gotten caught doing something wrong but was truly regretful about it. For a moment, Jules felt sorry for him.

"I'm sorry. It wasn't a lie. I was just trying to get some more time…"

"More time? Why?" She was confused. Why would he need more time, and why had he lied about the inspection in the first place? He could have just told her it was going to take more time. That seemed reasonable for a loan. "Is there a problem with the loan going through?"

"Why don't you sit down, and we can talk?" He put his hand out to take her arm, and she jerked away.

"I don't want to sit and talk. I want to know about the loan."

Nick sighed. "Well, there was a snag with the loan, but I'm working on it. I apologize about the inspection thing. I guess I shouldn't have said that, but I didn't know how to tell you there was a snag."

Jules made a face. How dumb was that? He didn't know how to tell her? She sensed there was more going on, but what? "We're not getting the loan, are we?"

"I didn't say that. It just hit a roadblock, but I'm working on it."

"But there's a problem?"

"Yes, but I think I can get it to go through."

"Think? Ughh… that's just great. We just hired a carpenter and bought things for the motel rooms, and now we might not have money. Perfect!" She threw her hands up in exasperation then opened her mouth to say more but realized she had no more to say. She spun on her heel and stormed off. She felt depleted, depressed. She didn't know if she was angrier at the lie or at feeling foolish that she'd thought she and Nick could become friends, or maybe even something more.

NICK SIGHED AND WENT BACK BEHIND HIS DESK, ignoring Louanne's raised-brow look from the teller window.

On his desk sat the application for the Beach-comber Motel loan. Corporate had kicked it back, and he was reworking some terms. It turned out that the loan was problematic and not only because Gramps had a stick in his craw about Jules's grandmother. Since there had been no income for decades, the bank saw it as a high risk, especially taking the bad credit of the debtors into account. Nick was trying to work around that, but he was going to have to go out on a limb and give a guarantee that might come back to bite him.

Gramps would not be happy when he found out.

All Nick's life, he'd done things for Gramps. Maybe it was about time he did something for himself.

Why had he panicked and lied about the inspection? It was stupid, stupid, stupid! He'd hoped maybe the loan would come through before anyone found out, and the inspection was something that would be needed anyway.

But even if he'd messed things up with Jules, the loan for the motel wouldn't be for nothing. The town needed that motel. Without it, there was no place for tourists to stay. And with no place for them to stay, there was no way for the town to thrive. Nick loved Shell Cove, and he wanted, more than anything, for the town to prosper. The town needed the Beachcomber Motel, and he needed the town. Even if Jules might never speak to him again.

He smiled when he thought of the flash of anger in her brown eyes, the flush on her cheeks. It had made her even more attractive, even though it had been directed at him in a negative way.

Guaranteeing the loan would be a big risk, but earning back Jules's trust, and giving the town something it desperately needed, was worth it.

❦

Rose pulled into the bank parking lot just as Jules was storming out.

"Oh my, she looks angry," Pearl said as they watched her get into her car and slam the door.

"Must be a tiff with Nick. Get your money ready because I think I might be about to win a bet." Leena watched Jules speed off.

"Not so fast." Rose pulled into her favorite parking spot in the first row from the door. "It's probably just a little misunderstanding. Things will settle down."

"Hmm, maybe," Leena said.

Pearl smoothed her blouse and looked into the bank. "If Nick is anything like his grandfather, he might turn into an old crab, so it might be in Jules's best interest to cut him loose now, before she gets too serious."

"You seem to be mentioning Henry a lot lately," Rose said.

"I am not. It's just hard to avoid when talking about Nick."

"Henry did used to be a lot of fun," Leena said. "We all used to be friends. Maybe we should try to bring him out of his gloom."

"I think he's been gloomy too long for that," Rose said.

"Started right before Rena left," Leena observed. "At first I thought she was going to be the thing that perked him up after his grief from his wife passing, but apparently that wasn't meant to be."

"I wonder what really happened between them. They were such good friends. I thought they might become more." Pearl's voice was wistful.

"Oh well, water under the bridge now and so long ago that doesn't excuse him for ignoring us and letting our friendship die out," Leena said.

"True, but still, maybe we should make the first overture." Rose's thoughts drifted back two years before. All of them except Rena had lived in Shell Cove their entire lives, and they'd been close to Henry at one time.

Rena had moved in later, when she bought the Beachcomber after her husband died. It hadn't taken her long to fit into the group of locals, though, and she and Henry had had a special relationship, or at least Rose had thought it was special. Now most of the old gang was gone, which was why it might be important to reconnect with Henry.

"That might be nice," Pearl said.

"He'll probably just tell us to beat it," Leena said. "His pretentious Cadillac isn't in the executive lot. Let's go deposit our Social Security checks before he gets here. I'm in a good mood and don't need him bringing me down today."

CHAPTER TWENTY

*M*addie liked Cassie, so she stood at the counter to sip her coffee so they could chat. She wanted to get her take on the town and see if she had any ideas for events that could bring people back to Shell Cove.

Their chat was interrupted when a fortyish-year-old woman in a power suit came rushing in, barking into her phone. "How could they just pull the permit from us? We have a show to put on!" The woman frowned as she listened to the answer. "No, we need a seaside town. We already have the advertising paid for and lined up with graphics of oceans and beaches."

Apparently, the woman was putting on some sort of event that needed a seaside town, and it sounded like she just had her venue canceled. Maddie was all ears.

The woman's voice became more exasperated as

she spoke. "It's too late to get another town to take us on. You know how long it takes those boards to meet and decide." She sighed, her eyes drifting about as she sniffed the air. "Though, this one does have a cute cafe shop and smells like decent coffee." The woman glanced over at Cassie and mouthed, "Café Americano."

Cassie got right to work.

"I don't know. The town is a bit dilapidated. I don't know the name of it. Shell something …" The woman let her voice trail off.

"Shell Cove," Maddie supplied. "And it's not really dilapidated. We're in the middle of renovating it."

The woman's gaze flicked from the street to Maddie. She spoke into the phone. "I'll call you back later, Evie."

"Sorry, I couldn't help but overhear." Maddie stuck out her hand. "Maddie Montgomery."

The woman responded with a firm handshake. "Marilyn Bryant."

"Sounds like you have some trouble finding a town to host your event." Cassie slid the cup of dark brew across the counter to Marilyn. "It's on the house."

"Thanks." Marilyn took a sip and closed her eyes. "Delicious." She opened them again and sighed. "I run the *Great New England Baking Contest* show. Maybe you've heard of it?"

Heard of it? Maddie was a big fan. "Yes, I watch it

all the time. Oh, you're having a contest here in a town on the coast?"

"Yeah, it's called Pie in the Sky." Marilyn laughed. "It's about pies, naturally. Anyway, we were supposed to start filming next week in Birch Bay, but I'm suddenly finding out that something went wrong, and the town is not allowing the filming. We have everything set, our contestants lined up, and now no place to have the contest."

"So you're looking for another coastal town?" Maddie felt her heartbeat pick up speed.

"Yeah, well, one who can pull it together on short notice." Marilyn took another sip of her coffee.

"We can," Maddie blurted. "I'm in charge of event planning here in Shell Cove, and we can approve it really quickly."

She glanced at Cassie, who was just staring at her behind the counter.

Marilyn looked out into the street, her expression doubtful. "Well, we usually set up somewhere more quaint."

"Oh, we can be quaint. Don't let those boarded-up windows fool you. Like I said, we're in the midst of renovating, and that's just part of it. We'll have it all spruced up by next week. We could speed it up for your schedule, though." Maddie hoped she didn't sound overeager, but she couldn't help the excitement bubbling up inside her.

That could be their big break. It was perfect. The event would attract a lot of people. The television show would put their name on the map, and they wouldn't have to pay a dime for advertising.

"You can?" Marilyn took another sip of coffee and looked to Cassie for verification of Maddie's claim.

Cassie was frozen, her gaze darting from Maddie to Marilyn to the street. Maddie widened her eyes at Cassie and mentally willed her to play along.

Cassie cleared her throat. "Yeah. Yep. We're fixing it all up. Going to be flowers and new awnings and everything. You just caught us on a bad day. It's going to be done by Monday for sure."

Marilyn tapped her shiny red nails on the counter as she gazed out into the street, considering their offer. "If that's all true, it could work, but we need a venue, a building that could accommodate the judging area, display area, and of course, kitchens to bake the pies in."

"We have that." Cassie was getting excited too. "The old donut factory. It's large enough and has a ton of ovens and a big kitchen, and it's on the pier—such a gorgeous location."

Maddie knew the building. It appeared as if it had been empty for some time and would need quite a bit of sprucing. Did it even still have the equipment inside? For all she knew, it was full of rotting wood, holes, and pigeons, but she wasn't about to tell Marilyn that.

"Can I check the place out?" Marilyn asked.

"Yes, of course. I'll find out how to get in and call you later?" Maddie didn't dare breathe, awaiting her answer. If she was going to take the time to check it out, then there was hope she would consider having the baking contest here.

"Sounds good." They exchanged contact info, and Marilyn left.

Maddie turned to Cassie. "I can't believe that just happened. This could be the thing that we need for this town and my motel." She scrolled through her contacts. She needed to get in touch with the welcome-wagon ladies pronto. She would need their help and the help of the whole town to pull this off.

CHAPTER TWENTY-ONE

Gina tried to form the dough in her hand into a ball, but all it did was crumble into little pieces and fall onto the flour-strewn counter. She pushed aside the pile of mixing bowls, measuring cups, and ingredients and spread some more flour on the piece of waxed paper she was using to roll out the dough.

The recipe had said the dough was supposed to be formed into a ball, but this dough wasn't complying. Her heart sunk. Just like Hugh had always told her, she wasn't good at anything. She tried to remember Gram's instructions on dough. Did she put more water in if it was crumbly or more flour? Gina couldn't remember.

Maddie came rushing in, bubbling over with excitement. "There's a baking show, and they're going to come to town, and it's perfect for—" She stopped speaking midsentence, her mouth open as she stared at the mess on the counter. "What are you doing?"

"I'm trying to make a pie, you know, because it was Gram's specialty, but it's not working out very well."

Maddie pointed at the crumbled pieces of dough. "Is it supposed to be like that?"

"No, it's supposed to be in a ball."

"Sorry. I don't have any idea how to bake, so I can't help," Maddie said. "But did you hear what I said? I ran into a woman in the coffee shop, and she could be the solution to all our problems."

"How so?" Gina turned from the dough disaster, eager to hear what Maddie had to say, though she didn't exactly know why she was eager, because she still intended to go home as soon as possible. Not that she had an actual house to go to anymore. But Boston was home, not there. In Boston she had friends... well, the two who were left "on her side" after Hugh disappeared. And she had her life, which consisted of... not much of anything since her business was dead and... well, okay maybe there really wasn't that much for her in Boston after all.

She listened as Maddie told her about running into Marilyn at the coffee shop and her dilemma with the baking contest.

"That sounds like it would be perfect," Gina agreed.

"I know, right? I have a message into the welcome-wagon ladies, and they're coming in two hours. This could be just what we need."

Jules came in through the lobby, her expression the exact opposite of Maddie's. Obviously things weren't going as well for her as they were for her cousin.

Maddie was oblivious to Jules's mood. She bubbled over with excitement as she repeated her explanation to Jules about the baking contest that needed a new town.

"And the best part is, if the people come, they're going to need a place to stay. We could rent them motel rooms."

Gina had a momentary panic. "Rent them? They're not really quite ready."

"But we could get them ready quickly. I know we don't have a lot of cash, but maybe we should charge some of it. We know that loan's coming soon."

"Sorry, guys. The loan isn't coming soon," Jules cut in.

Maddie's bubbly mood dimmed quickly. "What do you mean?"

"I just came from the bank, and Nick lied about the inspection," Jules said.

"I thought the inspector acted kind of weird about that, and it seemed odd that we'd need one," Gina admitted. She hadn't wanted to question Nick because maybe people did things weird in small towns. She'd never heard of such a thing in all her years of selling real estate, but she'd worked with residential homes.

"Yep. So he lied about that to buy time because there's some kind of problem."

"Now, wait a minute," Maddie said. "He didn't say we're definitely not getting a loan. He just said there's a problem?"

Jules shrugged. "He didn't say we were getting it either. And to tell you the truth, I wouldn't trust anything he did say about it."

Gina leaned against the counter, crossing her arms against her chest, oblivious to the fact that it got flour all over her shirt. "That's smart. Some men can never be trusted." Though she hadn't admitted it to her cousins, she knew from experience with Hugh.

Maddie held up her hands. "Okay, okay. So there's a snafu with the loan, but that doesn't mean we should give up on this opportunity. If they come to town, they'll be paying for the rooms. We'll be generating our own money, and the show will give this town the attention it needs. It's a popular show, and we won't have to pay a cent for advertising."

"But the hotel isn't in good condition. We have a hole in the porch, and everything's still under tarps," Jules said.

"We can fix that easily. Come on. Let's go outside and see what Dex has going on. We can ask how long he'll take to fix that hole in the porch. And the rooms weren't that bad. It won't be hard to fix them up."

"But we don't know what kinds of repairs they'll need. We just looked at the surface," Gina said.

"We can look further. Maybe we can have Dex help us out. Let's go find him and see if we can get this rolling. The welcome-wagon ladies will be here in two hours, and I want to have something specific to tell them."

Gina looked at the mess around her. "You guys go ahead. I'll clean this up and catch up with you later."

"Gina was baking?" Jules asked as she and Maddie walked around the side of the motel. "Something's fishy about that."

"Well, she did say she wanted to make pies like Gram."

"Huh, odd. I don't picture her as the type to bake."

Maddie slowed down and faced her cousin. "Me either. I don't think she's done much baking or cleaning, or work even, since we left the Surfstone Motel, but I think maybe she's in a bad place now. I mean, why do you think she sold her car?"

Jules glanced at the blue Honda parked a few spaces away from her own car. "Like she said, it had bad memories."

Maddie shook her head. "I don't know. It seems like she would buy something more expensive and brand-new if she had money. I think there might be more to her divorce than she's letting on. Maybe we should try to be kinder to her."

Jules snorted. "Yeah, right. She's got all that money and barely offered to chip in, and we should be kind to her?"

"Does she have money?" Maddie glanced at the car. "Maybe things are not as she is making them out to be."

"Oh, so she's lying. That figures," Jules said. "A leopard doesn't change its spots."

Maddie touched her arm, her expression full of kindness. It was just like her cousin to always think of others and not hold a grudge. Jules felt ashamed. Maybe she should try to be kinder.

"Maybe she's not really lying. Maybe she's embarrassed or hurt or even scared. She did pitch in money after she sold her car, and she's trying to make a dish for the town meeting. She's changing," Maddie said.

Jules shrugged. "I suppose."

Maddie continued around the side of the house toward the hammering noises of Dex working on the porch. "I've noticed you two aren't arguing about things like usual."

"That doesn't mean we'll be close," Jules said, but Maddie could tell from the tone of Jules's voice and the look on her face that it didn't mean they wouldn't be close either.

She was gaining ground on her mission to bring her cousins together. She glanced up at the sky as if to get Gram's approval. Looking up at the sky, however, turned out to be a problem because she immediately tripped over something on the ground. Strong hands caught her just before she face-planted. She jumped back, looking down to see what she had tripped over. A hammer. She looked up into Dex's smiling green eyes, furious.

"You shouldn't leave your tools lying around," she said, exasperated that he was so disorganized. Looking around the area, she could see tools everywhere. Planks of wood lay strewn about, and sawhorses were set with no apparent thought to organization.

"Whoa, slow down there. Why the scowl?" Dex asked. "You're usually Miss Sunshine."

Miss Sunshine? Maddie had been accused of being overly optimistic and too cheery before, but no one had ever called her a name about it. It didn't help that Jules barked out a laugh beside her.

"That name is perfect," Jules said.

"It is not." Maddie glared at her cousin.

"Okay." Dex held up his hands, still smiling. "Sorry, but this will cheer you up. Come check it out. The hole is fixed."

On the porch, rows of new boards had been placed where the rotted ones had been. The porch looked usable again, which was good, considering they might have guests sooner than they thought.

"Wow, nice work," Jules said.

"Thanks. I can start on that siding tomorrow." Dex picked up the hammer Maddie had tripped over.

"Actually, we have something else," Maddie said. "We might have some guests soon and need to assess the rooms to see if they have any structural issues. I mean, they look okay, but I'd like someone to take a closer look."

"Guests?" Dex asked.

"Yeah." Maddie told him about the event that could be coming to town.

"Wow, cool," he said. "But how are you going to get the town spruced up before Monday?"

"Good question." Maddie sounded nervous about the project for the first time. "I'm hoping that's something your grandmother can help me with."

CHAPTER TWENTY-TWO

*P*earl frowned at the crumbled balls of dough in the trash. "What is this mess?"

"Dough." Gina's expression was glum as she looked into the garbage.

They were in the kitchen of the Beachcomber and the welcome-wagon ladies had just arrived to discuss how they could pull off the opportunity of bringing the *Great New England Baking Contest* show to the town.

"Looks too dry. It needs some water." Pearl pushed her glasses up on her nose and squinted at Gina. "Were you making pie?"

Gina flushed. "I thought I'd try because Gram taught me, but it turns out I'm no good at it."

"Nonsense!" Pearl said. "You just need some practice. Your grandmother had recipes somewhere. That's what made her pies special."

"She wouldn't tell us what she put in the crust. She guarded them like state secrets," Leena said.

"Which was fine by me. I'd rather have her cook them and me eat them." Rose's joke got a chuckle from everyone.

"Did you guys see any recipes?" Maddie had looked around the kitchen to familiarize herself with what they had, and she hadn't seen any cookbooks or recipe files.

"Nope," Jules and Gina answered.

"But she hasn't been here in decades. If she had recipes, she probably took them with her. They might be in her house," Jules said.

"Cousin Tina is still sorting through Gram's things. I can message her if the recipes are important." Maddie glanced at Gina to see if they were.

"Oh no, I was just messing around." Gina tried to sound disinterested, but Maddie got the feeling that somehow those pies had become important to her. She made a mental note to message Tina anyway.

"Okay, so." Rose rubbed her hands together. "About this baking contest. I agree it's a perfect opportunity, and Cassie mentioned the donut shop would be the perfect place to host it."

The ladies had already heard all about the contest downtown. News spread fast in a small town.

"And what about the motel?" Leena asked. "These people will need someplace to stay."

Jules sighed. "We thought of that, but it turns out

the loan might not go through, so we're not exactly sure what to do about that."

"Sure we are," Maddie cut in. "We have some money saved and are going to spruce up the rooms. Dex finished the porch, so it's safe, and we had him look over the rooms to make sure there was nothing that needed immediate attention."

Rose smiled. "And how are you girls getting along with Dex?"

Jules smirked. "Maddie's getting along with him great."

"He sure is a charmer." Pearl gave Maddie a knowing smile.

"He's impossible. So disorganized. I don't think we're on the same page at all." Maddie looked out the window to make sure Dex had picked up his mess, as he'd promised. She had to admit he'd done a good job on the porch, and it had been nice of him to inspect the rooms, but she was glad he was out of her hair. She wanted to make friends in Shell Cove, but she doubted Dex would be one of them, even if he did have a charming smile.

"Tell us more about the loan," Leena told Jules.

Jules sighed. "It turns out Nick at the bank isn't exactly a straight shooter. The loan has some problems."

Pearl clucked. "I bet his grandfather is behind that."

Jules frowned. "Why do you say that?"

"Henry can be a jerk," Pearl said. "Maybe I should have a talk with him."

"You'd probably make things worse," Rose said.

"I think this was all on Nick. He lied about the inspection too. Luckily the motel passed," Jules said.

"It turns out that was a blessing in disguise." Maddie could tell Jules was trying not to let on how upset she was about Nick lying. "Nick did us a favor, really. The motel is already approved if we get guests for the contest."

"You can thank Dex for that," Gina pointed out, to Maddie's dismay. "Because he knew Ryan, he was able to show him the work being done and get his approval."

"Back to the contest," Rose said. "I'm going to call a town meeting. I think we can get most of the people on board with this. Hopefully we'll get lots of volunteers to clean up Main Street, take down the plywood from the boarded-up shops, maybe even get some flowers planted."

"Maybe Gina can bring a pie. It would be appropriate, considering the contest," Pearl said.

Judging by the look on Gina's face, Maddie didn't think she wanted to.

"Everyone needs to bring a dish," Leena reminded them. "That's how we get people to come."

"We'll bring something. Maybe not a pie, but something good." Hopefully it would be better than the fruit kebabs. Maddie felt a rush of excitement. If Rose thought it was possible, maybe she dared to hope.

"Okay now, what about the venue, the old donut shop? That might take a lot of work," Leena said.

"I drove by on the way back here," Maddie said. "It doesn't look too bad from the outside, but we need to get in there and check it out before I show it to Marilyn."

"No problem." Rose pulled a key out of her pocket. "I know the owner. Shall we go take a look right now?"

CHAPTER TWENTY-THREE

There was a lot of work to be done, so Pearl and Leena went to arrange the town meeting and spread the word while Jules took Rose to the donut shop on the pier in her car. Jules was surprised to discover that Dex was already taking the boards off the windows.

"Hi, Dex. What brings you here?" she asked.

Dex nodded toward Rose. "Gram mentioned that they were thinking of using this for that baking show and asked if I'd come and remove the boarded windows. It won't make a very good presentation with the windows blocked off." He peered over Jules's shoulder, as if looking for someone. "Is Miss Sunshine with you?"

Jules laughed. "No, she's back at the motel."

Rose raised her eyebrow. "Miss Sunshine?"

"He's talking about Maddie."

Rose laughed. "Oh, how interesting. Shall we go inside?"

She handed the key to Jules. Jules held her breath as she put the key into the lock, worried about what she might find inside. Would it be a complete wreck and unfit to even show to Marilyn?

It wasn't a wreck. In fact she was pleasantly surprised that it was in pretty good condition.

"It looks just like it did on the last day of business." Rose stood in the middle of the space. The shop was large with dozens of booths and a long counter in the back. As they walked through, they didn't notice any major problems.

The black-and-white tile floor was in good condition. The countertop looked intact under the thick layer of dust. Even the booths seemed to only have minor wear. And the view was fantastic.

"I'll call my cleaning lady. She can come tonight and get this place spic and span for tomorrow." Rose whipped out her phone.

"Thanks. I appreciate that." Jules walked along the booths toward the kitchen. "I wonder if the equipment still works. That would be important. How long has this place been shut down?"

Rose pressed her lips together. "Oh, about five years. They held out for a very long time. But as you can see, it's set up for a high volume of donuts. Back before the highway moved, we would have dozens of people come here. It was one of the attractions, and they would make fresh donuts of all different flavors. But when the highway moved and the tourist trade diminished, there really wasn't enough demand for donuts with just our locals. Ellie held out for as long as she could, but she eventually had to shut down."

The kitchen, though dusty, was gleaming in stainless steel equipment, commercial ovens, refrigerators, and stainless steel worktables. Jules opened one of the refrigerators, and the light came on.

"It still has electricity." She was surprised.

"Ellie kept the electricity on. It doesn't cost much with nobody using the place, and she always said she wanted to be ready to open at a moment's notice, just in case the tourists came back."

Jules looked around, mentally assessing the work that needed to be done. If the cleaning lady came in that night, she would be able to show it to Marilyn tomorrow.

"What's going on in there?" A vaguely familiar voice sounded outside.

Jules recognized the crotchety tone. It was Nick's grandfather.

Rose recognized it, too, apparently. She pressed her lips together and glanced out the window. "It's Henry."

Rose opened the door. "Hello, Henry. Nice to see you."

Henry scowled. "You, too, Rose. What's going on?"

"The *New England Baking Contest* is considering Shell Cove for their next show. I'm surprised you haven't heard. It's all over town."

"I haven't," Henry grouched. "What's that got to do with the doughnut factory?"

Jules could have sworn Henry was avoiding looking at her.

"This is where it will be hosted. It's perfect, and it could be very good for the town. It could bring a lot of tourists and get our name out there again," Rose said. "It could be good for the bank too."

"Harrumph. We'll see if that happens." Henry didn't sound optimistic.

"You remember Jules." Rose motioned toward Jules. "She applied for a loan for the Beachcomber Motel."

Henry looked at her then. She was expecting to see contempt because clearly the guy didn't like her, but instead, she saw a vulnerability that surprised her and a bit of sadness.

She bit back her sarcastic comment. "Nice to see you again."

He nodded a greeting. "The Beachcomber is in bad shape. A loan might not be a good investment for the bank."

Jules folded her arms over her chest. "So I've heard."

Henry stared at her, his sour expression turning soft.

"But don't judge my grandson too harshly. Sometimes things may be out of his control."

Jules faltered. What was the old guy saying? That it wasn't Nick's fault about the loan? But still, he'd lied to her about the inspection. That was his fault.

"Now, Henry, you know that motel is important for the town. If the baking show comes, it could change everything, then the motel would be a very good investment. You used to be a big champion for the town," Rose said.

"There are a lot of things that used to be. Those things are in the past." Henry looked them up and down "Good day." With a backward glance at the building, he shuffled off toward the parking lot.

Jules turned to Rose. "What was that about?"

"A long time ago, Henry was a nice guy. He was fun. But when his wife died, he hardened. It was to be expected for a while. He was grieving."

"I don't think he likes me, which doesn't bode well for the loan," Jules said.

"No, that's not it. Henry and your grandmother were close, but something happened," Rose said.

"What?"

"No one is sure. I thought maybe they would have a romance. And for a time, he seemed very happy."

"But?" Jules questioned.

"But then Rena left town. The highway had been moved, and tourists dried up. Rena had to close the motel, and she had another one up the coast to tend to."

"So you think Henry has a grudge against the motel or me?" Jules asked.

"You look like your grandmother. It's probably a reminder of what could have been."

"But that was decades ago. Who holds a grudge for so long?"

"Tell me about it. Some people take a long time to get over things, but let's not focus on that. We have a lot of work to do if the contest is coming to town, and you'll be able to prove to Henry that the motel will earn an income because you're going to have a lot of guests."

"Yeah, and if they want to start on Monday, it looks like we're going to be very busy getting the motel ready."

Jules glanced outside to see Henry moving slowly toward an old white Cadillac. The thing must have been twenty years old. Somehow it suited him.

He turned and looked at her, their eyes locking. Maybe the old guy wasn't so bad. He didn't seem crotchety or mean like she'd thought. He just seemed sad and remorseful. But just because her attitude toward him was softening didn't mean it was going to soften toward his grandson.

CHAPTER TWENTY-FOUR

Gina scoured the entire motel for her grandmother's recipes but came up empty. There was still no word from Hugh, and she'd exhausted all the friends and friends of friends who might know where he was. She was starting to think she was going to have to figure out how to live on what she had, which was basically nothing. Unfortunately, she had no skills or job prospects—except maybe the motel. And somehow the thought of staying there didn't seem so unpleasant anymore.

"Promise me you'll learn to enjoy the simple things." Gram's voice came back to her, bringing a tight smile to her lips.

But what exactly had she meant by simple? Certainly no lavish houses, fancy cars, maids, or cooks, like Gina had grown accustomed to. She'd once thought those essential, but the truth was she hadn't even missed them since she'd been in Shell Cove. She had enjoyed simpler things.

Since coming to the motel, she enjoyed the beach, memories of her grandmother, the satisfaction of trying to create something with her own hands, and the hard work she'd put into the motel. Oddly, she was looking forward to decorating the motel and excited that the pie contest might bring them guests. Could this have been what her grandmother meant all along?

In the kitchen, Maddie was at the table, her day planner open and lists and sheets spread in front of her. Jules was fiddling with the coffee maker, even though it was suppertime.

Gina almost offered to help. She'd gotten the operation of Mr. Coffee down to a science, but something made her hold back. She felt selfish about that. Jules wasn't that bad. And even though she'd fostered a grudge against her cousin for years, she could feel the importance of it fading. It was as if the Beachcomber Motel was softening her, changing her.

"Do you guys want something for supper?" Gina asked.

They'd taken to making sandwiches or getting take-out, since none of them could cook.

"Let's get pizza." Maddie pointed to the papers on

the table "I'm working on a plan. We can discuss it over slices."

"Sounds good." Gina pulled up the app for the pizza place in town. It was a little greasy for her liking, but it was the only one around.

She knew they would all want onion and green pepper, so she ordered a large for them to split. She'd gotten a fondness for pizza over the past week. Funny. She didn't even miss the fancy meals she'd been used to when married.

"So the donut shop was in good shape?" she asked after placing the order.

"Much better than I expected." Jules filled a mug with dark coffee from the machine then added a generous amount of milk. "It still has electricity, and I checked the ovens and fridge, and everything works. It would be perfect for the contest. Rose has her cleaning lady coming in to spruce it up. And I made an appointment with Marilyn to show it to her tomorrow morning."

"That's why we need to get on this right away. If she accepts, then we won't have much time to get the motel rooms ready." Maddie tapped the paperwork on the table.

"If they'll even be staying in the motel," Gina said cautiously as she sat.

Maddie smiled. "Where else would they stay? The

next hotel is almost an hour away. And we have the room. It's perfect."

Gina was excited about the prospect of guests. She wasn't sure why, because guests entailed things like cleaning and laundry, and those weren't things she was used to doing. But those were simple things, right? Maybe Gram had been onto something, because she was looking forward to all of that.

The pizza came, and they got to work. Maddie had already organized things in her head, so she was able to lead them through the discussion quickly. They decided to load up the shopping cart at the online stores where they wanted to buy the decor for the rooms, then they could simply click the Buy button if things worked out.

"Two-day delivery. Marilyn will make a quick decision, since the contest starts Monday, so if it's a go, we'll order right away and get the items here on time."

While they were waiting for that, they could work on the building exterior, as planned already. It was starting to look good. And since Marilyn knew they were revitalizing the town, the renovations wouldn't be off-putting.

"And, of course, we'll get all the porch furniture out, buy some hanging plants and some hostas or shrubs to spruce up the front area." Maddie sat back and grabbed another slice, folding it around her index finger before taking a bite. "We should take a quick inventory of the rooms and see if there's anything we need to grab from the storeroom that can be used to replace any broken or missing pieces."

Jules wiped greasy fingers on a napkin. "And what about the rooms? How many do you think they'll need? We're already taking up three of them."

"We need to rent as many as they want, so we might have to bunk together. Room ten has the two queens. We could share it." Maddie looked hopefully between Gina and Jules.

Surely she didn't expect Gina to share with Jules? Gina was finding Jules to be more tolerable than she'd first thought, but she still didn't want to get that chummy.

Apparently, Jules felt the same. "I'll bunk in there with you," she said to Maddie. "But I don't know if all three of us can fit."

"I can bunk in the storage room," Gina blurted out.

"You will?" Maddie scrunched up her face as if the thought were distasteful.

The room wasn't that bad, and Gina kind of liked the idea. "There's already an extra bed in there, and it's not so bad. Once we move the porch furniture out, there will be plenty of room. And besides, it's only temporary, and I'll be near the lobby in case the guests need something." Gina hoped she wasn't making it sound too pleasant. She didn't want to risk either one of them wanting to move in there too.

As they finalized their plans, an unwanted feeling of

optimism bubbled up inside her. Maybe Maddie was rubbing off on her, and it was only temporary, but for the first time in a long time, she was looking forward to the future.

CHAPTER TWENTY-FIVE

*M*addie met Marilyn at the shop early the next morning. She had to admit it looked pretty good, at least from the outside. Since she hadn't come with Jules and Rose on the initial inspection, she'd only seen it in passing before, and her impression hadn't been favorable. Someone had done a lot of work, and having the plywood off the windows made a big difference. And it appeared as if someone had put a fresh coat of paint on the trim. Dex?

Jules had mentioned he'd been working on it. It was ambitious and thoughtful of him, though Rose probably instructed him to do it. She was glad there were no paint cans or tarps sprawled all over the place. At least he'd picked up after himself.

There on the pier, the smell of the ocean was refreshing, and the sound of the water below was soothing. Someone had put two giant pots of colorful flowers on either side of the door, which created a nice effect. Maddie made a mental note to do something similar in front of the Beachcomber's porch steps.

"This is a great spot." Marilyn turned to take in the view of the pier. It stretched out a hundred feet into the ocean with a bumped-out section in the middle for fishing. There were two older gentlemen in ball caps on there right then with lines in the water. The donut shop itself was at the very beginning of the pier next to the parking lot, so people didn't have to walk too far to get to it.

"It used to be an attraction." Maddie relayed what Jules had told her. "You know, one of those must-see places. It had the largest variety of donuts in the area."

"The location is good. And the parking lot right at the end of the pier is perfect, but let's see the inside. We don't have time to renovate something to suit our needs."

Maddie crossed her fingers and opened the door. The inside was spotless; Rose's cleaning lady deserved a raise. It had booths and a huge counter just like Jules had described.

"Not bad." Marilyn walked around slowly, running a finger over the tabletops. She stopped at the counter. "This might work as a judging station, and if we moved those tables out of the way, the competitors could stand right in front with their dishes during the critique."

So far so good, but the real test was the kitchen. "The kitchen's through here. I'm told all the appliances are in good working order."

Maddie was pleased to discover that the kitchen gleamed with stainless steel. There were plenty of commercial stoves and two fridges. Steel pantry shelves lined one wall.

"Not bad." Marilyn turned one of the stove knobs, and the burner clicked a few times, then lit. She moved to the fridges, opening them and looking inside. "I'm going to send some pictures to Stacy. She stocks the kitchen and coordinates the production. We'll see if she thinks this setup will work."

Maddie sent out positive vibes for Stacy to approve the setup while Marilyn walked around taking pictures. After she was done, she took another tour, stopping in various places and talking about how they could position this or that to meet their needs.

Finally, Marilyn's phone pinged, and Maddie held her breath.

"Stacy said the place looks perfect. I think we might be able to make this work." Marilyn sounded excited as she put her phone away. "But I am a little worried about the town. It still looks…"

"Don't worry." Maddie hurried to reassure her. "The town will be all fixed up by Monday. We're actually having a town meeting tonight to work out the details." Maddie tried to smile reassuringly, even though she had no idea if the townies would want to fix things up before Monday. She would do it herself if she had to.

"Okay, well, honestly I don't have much choice, so it's either go ahead or stop the entire production." Marilyn turned to look around the shop again. "If the town can rush through the required permits, I'll need to know who to rent this from. Oh, and the crew and contestants will need a place to stay. Is there any place closer than the Driftwood?"

The Driftwood was almost an hour away.

"How many people are we talking?"

Marilyn screwed up her face. "Let's see. There's the crew of five, me and five contestants."

Eleven people, which was perfect because that was exactly how many rooms they had empty at the Beachcomber once she and Jules moved in together and Gina moved to the storage room.

"No problem. I have the perfect place right down the road, and there's plenty of room for everyone."

CHAPTER TWENTY-SIX

*G*ina didn't remember pie making being so exhausting. Mixing the dough took muscles she never used, and rolling it out was an exercise in frustration when it kept separating at the edges. Gram had always done most of the work.

She still hadn't found any recipes, but a strawberry pie recipe from a Maine food column by Paula Anderson and Pearl's tip of adding water to the dough got her through. The sides of the crust weren't fluted evenly, and the top didn't have fancy designs like Gram used to make, but at least it was better than the fruit kebabs they'd brought to the prior town meeting.

She felt proud when she placed it on the table in between Cassie's cream cheese brownies and Deena's chocolate fudge before taking her seat in one of the folding chairs in the town hall.

At the front of the room, Rose clapped her hands, and the murmur of voices stopped as everyone took their seats.

"As you all have probably heard by now, the *Great New England Baking Contest* is coming to Shell Cove next week."

People murmured. Some clapped. A few looked skeptical.

"This will be great for the town and our businesses," Rose continued. "But there is one caveat. We need to get Main Street looking its best."

More murmuring and people shifting in their seats. Dwight, the grump from the first meeting, raised his hand. "How are we supposed to do that? It's only a few days away."

"Good old-fashioned elbow grease," Rose said as if it were the most fun one could have.

"I don't know," a woman said. "I have plans, and I'm not as young as I used to be."

Cassie Fox stood and looked over the crowd. "I'm young, and I can help you with the heavy lifting. My shop doesn't need much."

A woman with long, dark hair stood. Gina thought she'd seen her around town doing landscaping. "I'll donate the flowers. I can fill those giant pots on Main Street and the window boxes on the shops."

Rose beamed from her place behind the podium. "Thank you, Lorna. That's very generous."

The next few minutes had a flurry of townspeople discussing ideas and volunteering to help. By the time Rose called an end to the meeting, pretty much everyone in the room was on board with cleaning up the town and eager to get started. Even Dwight seemed optimistic.

Everyone rushed to the food table, including Gina. She couldn't wait to see what people thought of her pie.

JULES SCANNED THE CROWD AT THE TOWN MEETING. SHE wasn't looking for anyone in particular, certainly not Nick, but she was pleased to find that she recognized more faces than last time.

She was glad Nick wasn't one of them. He was probably too embarrassed to face her. His grandfather was there, though. He'd nodded to her politely then proceeded to avoid her. Oh well, at least the meeting had gone well, and the town was up for sprucing up the shops along the main street.

Things were looking up for the Beachcomber despite the uncertainty of the loan. With each passing day, Jules felt that their odds of actually getting it were dwindling, especially since she hadn't heard anything from Nick.

An update would have been nice, but if there was nothing to say because the loan had been denied, then she supposed he might not want to update her. But if it had been denied, wouldn't his grandfather have said something? No sense in dwelling on the negative.

Marilyn had booked the rooms at the Beachcomber, and they'd gotten a hefty deposit, which allowed them to pay the electric and gas bills and for all the supplies they'd ordered to decorate the rooms. The balance would pay Dex's bill. Jules didn't want to look any further than that. Best to take things one day at a time, she thought as she headed toward the food table, where Gina was hovering near her pie.

Gina had changed in the short time they'd been at the Beachcomber. She seemed more relaxed, less... annoying. But old wounds ran deep, and Jules still wasn't inclined to be besties with her. But maybe, just maybe, they could get past that, eventually. She still wasn't going to try any pie. The presentation was less than appealing, though she would refrain from saying that to Gina's face.

Jules grabbed a small plate and reached behind Pearl for a cream cheese brownie. Gina must have talked Pearl into tasting the pie because the older woman held a plate with a piece of it, her fork hovering over the slice as if she were trying to force herself to dig in.

Jules watches as Pearl forked off a tiny piece and put it in her mouth. She plastered on a smile as she swirled it around in her mouth. It looked like she was hiding a grimace, and when she finally managed to swallow it, she put the plate down.

"Well, that sure is savory." Pearl patted her lips with a napkin.

"Savory? It's strawberry pie!" Gina frowned at the pie before cutting off a sliver for herself and taking a bite. "Oh, I see what you mean."

"Maybe it needs more sugar or some spices," Pearl suggested. "Rena used to have a cinnamon crust she would make that was out of this world."

"I remember that crust." Rose eyed Gina's pie then saw Pearl's plate with most of the piece still on it and opted for coffee cake.

"Pie takes practice," Leena said. "I think things went better than expected tonight."

"Agreed." They all moved over to a corner of the room with their plates.

Rose nodded toward Maddie, who was busy talking to some shop owners. "Your cousin is a born organizer, a real asset to the town."

"Maybe she'll head up the chamber of commerce," Pearl said.

"Are you looking for someone to do that?" Gina asked.

"We will be if things work out." Rose wiped coffee cake crumbs from her lips. "Let's not get ahead of ourselves. We need to focus on how to capitalize on this baking contest. I've already seen more people driving around town since it was announced."

Pearl turned to Jules. "I heard the motel is booked with cast and crew of the show. I bet you get more inquiries from people who want to stay in town for it. The show is quite popular, and people generally flock to wherever it's being held."

"We're full, but that would be great just to know people want to stay there," Jules said, her gaze fixed on the door where Henry was just exiting.

As they watched, he glanced over at them and nodded before turning and leaving.

"Did he just nod at us?" Pearl asked.

"I thought I might have seen a ghost of a smile," Rose said.

Leena snorted. "I doubt it. He's still crotchety. I ran into him the other day, and his demeanor has not improved."

"I don't know," Jules said. "He seems more sad than crotchety, if you ask me."

Rose tossed her plate in the trash and brushed the crumbs off her shirt. "Let's not waste time worrying about him. We have a ton of work to do if we want to get this town fixed up by Monday."

HENRY FELT LIGHTER AS HE GOT IN HIS CAR IN THE parking lot of the town hall. He'd spent so many years thinking nothing could revive the town. It was difficult for his old brain to process the fact that maybe it could be restored. Maybe if this had happened years ago, Rena wouldn't have left without even saying goodbye. Funny that it took her granddaughters to make it happen.

His thoughts turned to Rose, Pearl, and Leena. They'd been friends once, even before Rena came to town, but in his bitterness, he'd broken ties with them. For the life of him, he couldn't really remember why. Had he been so deep in despair that he simply wanted to wallow in loneliness with only Nick for company?

Where had Nick gone today, anyway? He'd mentioned an errand out of town, but he'd seemed evasive and nervous, as if there was something he didn't want Henry to know. Could it be related to the loan for the Beachcomber? The other day, Rose and Jules had made it sound like the loan might still happen. But if that were true, it would mean that Nick was going behind his back. The thought of that made Henry smile. It was about time the boy put his neck on the line for something important to him.

As Henry drove away, he glanced back at the old meetinghouse. He could see in through the tall windows, and people were milling about, paper plates of food in their hands. The room had an energy of excitement, and for the first time in a long time, the people of Shell Cove appeared optimistic. His heart softened, and he felt a pang of longing when he spotted Rose, Leena, and Pearl standing in a tight group.

Things were changing in Shell Cove. Maybe it was time he changed too.

CHAPTER TWENTY-SEVEN

Maddie pulled the last T-shirt off the hanger, folded it neatly, and put it in the suitcase on the bed. She was only moving a few rooms down to bunk with Jules so they could rent more rooms to the guests, but she liked things to be neat and organized, as opposed to her cousin, who she'd seen walking past her room with a stack of clothing spilling from her arms.

At least she only had her clothes and a few personal items to move. She'd put most of her things in storage back home since she didn't know if things would work out in Shell Cove or not. Maddie hefted the suitcase off the bed and rolled it out toward her new room.

"I'll take this side of the closet, okay?" Jules was already hanging up her wrinkled shirts.

"Fine." Maddie looked around the room. It was a

little bigger than the one she'd had previously but more crowded, given the two beds. It was missing some artwork on one wall and needed interior painting, but they all needed that. "Do you think we'll be able to get these rooms painted in two days?"

"Maybe we could hire someone." Jules turned around and raised her eyebrows. "Like Dex."

Maddie's instinct was to say no. She didn't need his disorganized mess and annoying personality. But would the old paint cause them to get bad reviews about how the motel was outdated? "Maybe."

"I'm sure he'll be happy to defer payment again." Jules frowned. "But seeing as I haven't heard anything about the loan, maybe we shouldn't."

Maddie unzipped her suitcase and started putting her clothes away.

"It's going to be weird bunking together in here," Jules said from the bathroom.

Maddie glanced in to see that she'd cluttered up the sink with a toothbrush, hairbrush, and various lotions and bottles.

Maddie sighed. She was used to living by herself, and having Jules as a roommate was going to be trying, but she decided to put a positive spin on it. "It will be a challenge, but kind of like when we were kids and would stay with Gram. That used to be fun."

Jules sat on the bed, bouncing a bit to test it out. "Fun? We're not kids. But I guess we'll make do."

"We won't be spending much time in here anyway. I think we're going to be very busy fixing up the motel and tending to guests."

"Yeah, we should probably come up with a plan to make it run smoothly," Jules said.

Finished putting her clothes away, Maddie zipped up her suitcase and stowed it in the closet, then sat on the other bed facing her cousin. "Remember how we did it at the Surfstone? That process worked well."

At the other motel, they'd divided up the work to suit their skill sets. Maddie had taken care of social activities and events along with finances. Jules had taken care of customer relations, checking people in and answering questions, and Gina had figured out the back-end logistics like cleaning and making sure they were stocked with linens and so on.

Jules made a face. "I don't know. Gina isn't the same person she was back then. Being rich might have dulled her enthusiasm for work."

"Maybe, but seems like she's coming around. Don't you think?" Maddie asked.

Jules tilted her head to the left, as if considering the question. "I guess so. She did apply herself to making the pies, but I don't know. I get the impression she might not be as committed to this motel as we are."

Maddie had thought so, too, at first, but she was sure Gina was having a change of heart. And she sensed that Jules had also seen it. The relationship between the two of them was changing as well. If Maddie could just do something to push it in the right direction, she could fulfill her promise to her grandmother. And it wasn't just about the promise. Maddie wanted the cousins to get along.

"Come on. Let's go see how Gina is getting on in the storage room. We need to come up with a plan for renovating these rooms in time for the guests."

Renovating the rooms, that was the perfect activity. Getting them ready in time would take close teamwork, and Maddie had an idea on how she could force Jules and Gina to take the next step in healing their relationship.

GINA WAS JUST FLUFFING THE PILLOW ON HER BED WHEN Jules and Maddie appeared in the storage-room door. The pillows and sheets had all been sealed in plastic bags and were as fresh as new. Leave it to Gram to think of everything. Her foresight and care of the items at the Beachcomber had saved them time and money.

"Knock knock." Maddie came into the room and looked around. "Well, this looks homey."

Gina stood back and smiled. She'd pulled the bed over to one side under the only window in the storage area and had put a pretty comforter on the bed. She'd even arranged some old brocade pillows to lean against the headboard for good measure. She'd pulled one of the shelves along the side to make a divider. It wasn't like anything she was used to in her elaborate houses, but somehow it felt a lot more cozy and comfortable.

"This doesn't look half bad," Jules said.

"Thanks. How are things working out in your room?" Gina hoped they didn't get any ideas about moving in with her.

"Fine," Jules said noncommittally.

"It's going to be fun," Maddie chirped.

Jules turned away, pretending to inspect something on the shelves, but not before Gina caught her rolling her eyes. At least they were in agreement on the fact that Maddie's optimism could get tedious at times.

"Now that everything is moving forward, we need to figure out how to get this place presentable before the baking-show people check in. I was hoping we could talk about that tonight." Maddie pulled two chairs from a stack that had been in the corner of the room and sat them beside each other.

"Now? You don't have your day planner," Jules teased.

"Ha-ha." Maddie pulled a notepad out of her pocket. "Don't worry. I did come prepared. I figured we could talk while Gina finishes setting up her room."

"Okay, we do need to make a plan." Jules sat in the chair next to Maddie while Gina foraged on one of the shelves. She still needed some accessories to complete making her room feel like home.

"The comforters and accessories are being delivered first thing tomorrow," Maddie said.

"Oh, that reminds me," Jules said. "Dex is going to paint those two rooms. Rose messaged me that he volunteered."

The motel rooms had vintage grass-cloth wallpaper on one wall and paint on the others. They all needed a paint refresh with modern colors, but there wasn't time to do all of them before the guests came. Two of the rooms, though, had peeling wallpaper, so it was a must that they redo them right away.

"Dex? How much will that cost?" Maddie asked.

"Rose said he's doing it for free, part of volunteering for the town."

Gina turned around in time to see Jules cast a knowing look in Maddie's direction. Maddie was frowning as she looked at her list.

Gina had noticed Maddie and Dex had a certain chemistry. Maddie seemed intent on denying that. Gina wasn't sure why. Maybe her cousin had had a bad experience in the past like Gina had with Hugh. But Dex seemed nice, even though he was one of those charmers who usually ended up breaking girls's hearts. Maybe Maddie had had her heart broken one too many times already.

"I don't know if that's such a good idea. Doesn't it

take a while for the paint to dry?" Maddie asked. "We only have a couple of days before guests check in."

"It's latex paint, so we can get two coats up in eight hours. Dex is bringing a friend, so it should be no problem," Jules said.

Gina slipped in between two storage shelves while Maddie considered the paint situation. She didn't have an opinion and needed some more items to make her space cozy. She spotted a cute, round white side table with turned legs behind some boxes and pulled it out.

"I guess that will be okay," Maddie said finally as Gina emerged from behind the shelves and placed the table beside the bed.

It would be perfect to hold a glass of water and a book at night. She stood back to assess then moved it a few inches back toward the wall.

"Looks good." Jules seemed as surprised at herself for voicing the compliment as Gina was to hear it.

"Thanks." Gina glanced at her cousin, and she felt a truce starting to form. Did she want a truce? She would think about that later. Right then, she needed a lamp for that side table.

"So I was thinking we'll lay all the accessories out in one spot then do the rooms one at a time. I think that will make it go faster," Maddie said as Gina rummaged the shelves and boxes.

"Okay," Jules said. "We can work on the ones that aren't being painted, then by the time the painted rooms are ready, we'll know exactly where to put everything."

They'd decided earlier to rearrange the rooms, as they put on the new bedding and pillows, so that each room was a little different. Gina was looking forward to that. In her staging role for their real estate company, she'd developed a knack for figuring out where to place furniture and accessories, and it would be a nice challenge to figure out how to make each room slightly different.

She already had some ideas for bed placement and bureaus. It felt good to be doing something creative and productive—she'd spent too many years having other people do those things for her. She let her cousins make the plans as she poked through the boxes. There was a lot of stuff in there. Some of it brought up sweet memories of Gram. One old, tall cardboard box held a seahorse-shaped lamp that would be perfect for her bedside table.

She struggled to pull the lamp out, careful not to break it. Backing out from the space between two shelves, she heard Maddie say, "And you guys can work together on arranging the rooms while I get the plants for the porch from Lorna. She said she'd give us some."

Wait. Work together? Gina glanced at Jules, who looked as uncomfortable as she felt.

"We can split up the rooms," Jules suggested.

"Good idea." Gina put the lamp on the table. It looked perfect.

"Oh, I don't know if that will work," Maddie said. "It's going to take two people to rearrange the furniture. I was picturing that you could work together. You have different strengths in decorating that complement each other and will make a great team. Now won't that be fun?"

Gina turned to stare at Maddie. Surely she couldn't be serious. She knew about the deep rift between Gina and Jules. But the gleam in her cousin's eyes told Gina she was indeed serious. Maddie was up to something, and Gina doubted it was going to end up the way Maddie envisioned.

CHAPTER TWENTY-EIGHT

*J*ules awoke bright and early the next morning feeling optimistic. Perhaps she'd caught it from sharing the room with Maddie. They'd fallen asleep early, exhausted from the day of planning, moving, and working on the exterior painting project, which was almost done.

Maddie had arisen about a half hour ago. She'd thrown open the window, letting sunshine and sea air spill into the room, then rushed off to the kitchen, mumbling something about coffee.

Jules kicked the covers off and got out of bed. There was a lot to do that day, so she didn't waste any time, throwing on the T-shirt she'd worn the day before and bunching her hair into a ponytail before giving her teeth a quick brush and heading to the motel kitchen in the hopes that Maddie had mastered the ancient coffee machine. It wasn't as good as the coffee from Ocean Brew, but they didn't have time to run into town, so it would have to do.

She ran into Dex on the way over. He was carrying a tray of coffees from Ocean Brew.

"Good coffee saves the day!" Jules took the container he offered. "Thanks."

"I figured you guys might need some. Are your cousins around? I got one for everyone."

"Maddie is in the kitchen wrestling with our coffee maker right now. I'm sure she'll be delighted to give up on it and drink this."

She led him into the kitchen, where Maddie was standing at the counter. She had a pitcher of water in her hand and was muttering at the coffee maker, which sat with its lid up, as if sassing her back.

"I can't get this—" She turned, stopping midsentence when she saw Dex with the coffees. "Oh, hi."

"I picked these up on my way." Dex held the tray out to her, and Maddie selected a cup. "I didn't know what everyone preferred to drink, so I just got regular coffee."

"That's good. Better than this thing." Maddie gestured toward the coffee machine on the counter, which gave a gurgle as if resenting it was the subject of their conversation.

"You guys might want to invest in a K-Cup machine." Dex laid the tray on the table and picked out two coffees, holding one up. "This is for my helper, Riley, the one left is for Gina."

"That was really nice of you to bring those." Jules looked at Maddie to see if her attitude toward Dex had softened. She thought Maddie was a little overly critical with her assessment of him, and she could tell Dex was attracted. It was none of her business, but they would make a cute couple. Maybe Maddie's overdeveloped organizational skills could help him, and his apparent spontaneity could help her.

"Yeah. Thanks." Maddie gave him a quick look then turned to Jules. "I have to run into town and pick up the plants, but I was hoping you could help me uncover the wicker furniture in the lobby and put it out on the porch real quick. Gina isn't up yet."

"I can help," Dex volunteered.

Maddie looked like that was the last thing she wanted. "Umm oh, isn't that your helper?" She nodded toward the window, where they could see a tan truck pull into the parking lot.

"Oh yeah, he can help too." Dex looked at Maddie over the rim of his cup, apparently determined to help them.

"Fine. I mean we can do it on our own, but I suppose it will go faster if you help."

They rounded up Riley, and the four of them took the tarps off the wicker and hauled it out to the porch. Jules was pleased to discover that the furniture was in fine condition. It gave the porch an old-fashioned Victorian vibe—very cottage chic. The plants would add a nice finishing touch.

When they were just about done, the delivery of bedding and accessories came, and Jules felt her excitement ramping up. They were one step further to actually having paying guests. Sure, the motel still needed some things, but it was in decent shape. Her excitement was tinged with nervousness. Would the guests like it?

Jules started opening the boxes while Maddie fussed with the pillows, and Dex and Riley got started with the painting.

"He's not so bad." Jules nodded toward Dex, who was piling brushes, ladders, crumpled up tarps, and cans of paint outside one of the motel rooms.

Maddie barely glanced over. "I guess."

Jules inspected the items. The comforters were good quality, very puffy, and looked comfortable in soft colors of white with aqua and orange. The artwork of seashells, starfish, and crabs matched perfectly. The throw pillows were a nice touch, and the color-coordinated hand towels would give a pop to the bathrooms.

Jules organized them by theme. Starfish motif in one pile, shell motif in another, seahorses in a third. She made piles on the porch, already picturing how they would look in the rooms.

Gina appeared in the doorway, the coffee they'd left

on the kitchen table in her hand. Steam wafted out of the lid. She must have microwaved it.

"This is the bedding?" Gina inspected one of the comforters.

"Yeah, it's pretty nice."

"Good. I was worried." Gina's attention turned to Maddie, who was moving a wicker rocker from one side of the porch to the other. "I think maybe it will look best in the corner here." She pointed to a corner next to the house, and Maddie placed it there, then stood back.

"You're right. You're so much better at placement than I am." Maddie brushed her hands together. "Speaking of which, you two should get started on the rooms. I have to get into town."

Maddie bounced off, leaving Jules and Gina on the porch alone.

Jules was suddenly wary at the thought of working alone with Gina without Maddie as the buffer. But she took a deep breath and grabbed an armful of items for the first room. "Well, I guess we better get started."

Not even Gina could put a damper on her good mood that day.

MADDIE PEEKED AROUND THE CORNER OF THE PORCH, watching Jules and Gina as they worked on the rooms.

They seemed to be communicating, and neither of them had stormed off in a huff. So far, so good.

She'd spent the day cleaning up the lobby and arranging the plants Lorna had given her. The woman had been very generous, supplying her with five pots of dark-purple petunias, which now hung around the porch, their velvety purple flowers spilling out of the baskets and trailing toward the ground.

She'd also given Maddie two large pots of mixed flowers to put on either side of the steps and flats of impatiens to plant along the walkway. It had taken her most of the day to plant them, but it felt good to dig in the dirt, and when she stepped back to look at her handiwork, she was surprised at how much the addition of the flowers transformed the look of the motel from a neglected run-down building to a cozy motel that just might need a few touch-ups.

Ready for a break, she peeled her gardening gloves off and wiped sweat from her brow with the back of her hand. Her phone rang. It was Rose.

"Dex tells me things are looking good over at the motel."

"They are. It's shaping up nicely." Over at the rooms, Dex and Riley were just cleaning up. Jules and Gina were working on their last room, and Maddie supposed that later that night, they would finish the two rooms that just got painted.

"That's great," Rose said. "If you guys want to take

a break, you should see what's happening downtown. The girls and I are getting an ice cream. Come join us. You won't believe how nice it looks."

From her vantage point at the motel, Maddie could see a portion of the downtown area. She'd seen people busily moving about down there and noticed an awning getting replaced and a few sheets of plywood coming down, but she would love to see the whole effect.

"That sounds like a good idea. I'll get Gina and Jules, and we'll meet you there in about ten minutes."

She started toward the rooms, nodding at Dex, who was putting a ladder in his truck on the other side of the parking lot. She really should go over and thank him, but something about him made warning bells ding in her head, so she simply waved and continued past.

Gina and Jules were each on a different side of the bed, putting on a bedspread with a colorful seashell design. They each straightened their sides, and both stood back. They had managed to change the room from outdated and stuffy to new and cozy. Who knew that just some new bedding and accessories could accomplish that?

Maddie stopped in the doorway. "Hey, you guys want to take a break and head downtown? Rose says the town is looking great."

"Sure," Jules said. "We're done here anyway."

"It looks really fantastic," Maddie said. "You guys transformed it."

"We rearranged the bed and bureau so when you walk in, it looks more welcoming," Gina said.

"And the new bedding brightens it up," Jules added. "We should have thought to order new curtains. That's next on the list."

"Amazing! I knew you guys could do it," Maddie said.

Jules and Gina were practically beaming, and Maddie felt proud that she'd somehow had a hand in getting them to work together.

"Thanks. It was kind of fun." Gina held her fist out toward Jules. "To teamwork!"

Jules smiled and bumped Gina's fist. "Teamwork!"

Maddie could feel a bond forming between them. She'd fulfilled her promise to Gram, but somehow she felt that her job in Shell Cove wasn't done.

Gina and Jules looked as surprised at the fist bump as she was.

She didn't want them to overthink the gesture. "Okay, great. Let's get going. Rose mentioned something about ice cream."

CHAPTER TWENTY-NINE

"Wow, this place does look really different." Jules smiled as she scanned the shops on the main street of town. Just yesterday many of the windows had been boarded up with plywood, the window boxes held only dirt and twigs, and the street looked sad and unused.

Today, the plywood had been removed from the shops that weren't in business. Colorful flowers spilled out of every window box as well as the large planters on the sidewalk, and the streets had been swept clean.

The glass in the windows of every store gleamed, and it looked like someone had painted the trim on the outside. Even the stores that were closed had shed their look of abandonment with sparkling clean windows and large potted plants in front of the doors. The insides were mostly empty, but they could see a few old display cases and furniture that held a promise of businesses to come.

There were more people milling about than she'd ever seen. They were smiling, talking, laughing, and there was a festive vibe.

"How did you make out with the flowers?" Lorna Baxter stopped next to them. She held a vibrant-pink hanging plant in each hand.

"Excellent," Maddie said. "They make such a difference. Thank you so much for offering them. If you ever have relatives or friends who want to visit Shell Cove, we'll give you a big discount on rooms at the Beachcomber."

Lorna smiled. "Thanks. I might take you up on that. I guess I better go hang these. There are still a few more to put up." She headed off toward Ocean Brew, where Jules could see she'd already strategically hung two other plants along the front. Inside, the coffee shop was abuzz, with Cassie busy behind the counter and people sitting at the tables, sipping coffees and hot chocolates.

Everything was changing in Shell Cove. Even working with Gina to improve the motel rooms hadn't been as bad as she'd expected. Maybe it was time for her to let go of the past and think about the future, much like it seemed the town itself was doing right then.

"I think someone mentioned ice cream," Maddie said to Rose.

"Sully's makes the best ice cream." Pearl pointed to a small shop on the corner.

Jules was surprised she'd never noticed it with the bright-pink awning and giant ice cream cutout on the sidewalk in front.

"Has that been there the whole time?" Gina asked.

"Yep." Rose started toward it. "But they got a new awning today and haven't used the giant ice cream sign in a while, so it does look a little different."

They each got an ice cream and sat on the benches under an oak tree across the street from the candy store, Saltwater Sweets. The front window was packed with a mouthwatering display of candy ranging from fudge to caramel turtles to bark. White chocolate, dark chocolate, milk chocolate—they certainly had a wide variety.

Inside, a man in a white baker's shirt spread chocolate on a marble slab, and the owner, Deena, bustled around, fussing with the display cases. Jules remembered her from the town meetings.

"It's nice to see Deena taking pride in the shop again." Pearl had a kiddie cone upside down in a cup and was daintily spooning up tiny bits of ice cream.

Jules admired her restraint, but at that rate, it was going to take her all summer to eat it.

"After John died, she really went into a funk." Rose licked her pistachio cone then turned to Jules, Maddie, and Gina. "Saltwater Sweets has been an important business in this town for over a hundred years. Deena's great-grandmother started it with her secret chocolate recipe. Deena ran it with her husband for many years, but when he died, the light went out of her life, and she lost interest. The shop went downhill."

"It looks like she's found her light again," Leena said.

"I think that might have something to do with her new friend." Pearl raised her brows toward a tall, gray-haired man standing in the corner. Every so often, Deena would turn to him, as if asking his advice, and they would favor each other with a lingering smile.

"She did mention a new man in her life," Rose said. "I guess that can make one giddy."

"Gram!" Dex waved at them from across the street.

Jules's heart lurched when she saw that Nick was with him. She was sort of embarrassed about how she'd yelled at him about his lie. She still thought it was strange that he'd lied, but it had actually worked out well for them, considering they needed the permit in order for the *New England Baking Contest* to stay at the motel. The irony was that if Nick hadn't lied, they might not have gotten that permit in time.

She wished she hadn't lost her cool like that, but she didn't want to explore the thought that maybe she'd been madder about him betraying her trust because she thought they might be forming an important friendship than it was about the lie. Either way, she didn't have much to say to him, so she focused on her butter crunch ice cream while everyone greeted each other.

"I heard the motel is full up." Nick came to stand next to her.

"Yeah, it's great." Jules kept her eyes on the ice cream. She really didn't want to encourage him.

"I just wanted to apologize again for my stupid lie. I'm still trying to get that loan through for you."

"Thanks." Jules managed a small smile then dug back into her ice cream. Hopefully he would get the hint and leave.

"Come on, man, let's go check out the brew pub. Harley said he's got a new summer ale for us to try." Dex jerked his head toward the end of the street, where Jules supposed the brew pub must be.

"There's a brew pub?" Gina looked mildly interested, which was a surprise.

Jules pictured her to be more the champagne type. Her cousin was full of surprises that day.

"Sure. You ladies want to join us?" Dex's gaze lingered on Maddie.

"No!" Maddie and Jules said at the same time.

Dex looked confused at their insistent tone.

"We still have a lot of work to do at the motel. Probably not a good idea tonight," Gina said.

Dex nodded. "We'll do it some other time."

"Such nice young men," Pearl said as they walked off down the street.

"Wait until you see them in the brew pub. That might change your minds," Leena joked. "Especially with Lorelie out of town."

"Who's Lorelie?" Jules asked.

"Dex's girlfriend." Pearl made a face. "Not well suited, if you ask me."

"Did I sense you giving Nick the cold shoulder?" Rose asked.

"Was I?" Jules scooped up the last of her ice cream. "I guess I don't feel chatty when it comes to him."

Rose exchanged a glance with Pearl and Leena. Leena had a smirk on her face, and she tapped her purse in what looked like some secret signal to the other ladies.

"That's funny. The two of you looked pretty chummy the other day in Ocean Brew," Pearl said.

Jules shrugged. "Things change, I guess."

"Is it about the loan?" Rose asked. "What's going on with that?"

"Nothing, really. He says he's trying to push it through, but I guess there's some holdup."

"Maybe you won't need it." Pearl scooped up another speck of ice cream. The rest of them were done, and she still had over half of hers left. "The motel is booked, right?"

"Yeah, we had to bunk together." Maddie held out

her hand for the empty ice cream cups and stacked them.

"So you'll get money from that. Maybe it will hold you over, and maybe after this, more tourists will come." Pearl pulled her cup away from Maddie's grasp.

"Maybe." Jules glanced at her cousins. Would it be enough? Even though they'd spruced the motel up, it still needed some work, and if they wanted to truly update the rooms, they were going to have to spend some money.

Rose patted Jules's leg. "I'm sure Nick will come through. He hasn't soured on life like his grandfather. Yet."

Pearl swirled a tiny blob of ice cream around in her cup. "I don't think Henry has soured. He just needs closure."

"Ha! Well, where's he going to get that?" Leena asked.

Pearl shrugged. "I don't now, but we were close to him once. We should try to help. One shouldn't just abandon old friends."

Jules glanced at Gina. Was that what she and Gina had done? Abandoned old friends?

"We've tried to get him to come around." Leena sighed. "Maybe he just needs time."

"Maybe." Pearl dropped her spoon into her cup as if to signal she was done. The half that was left had turned to soup, and the cone was soggy. "Let that be a lesson to you girls. Don't hold on to old grudges, and don't forget to have fun!"

"That's right," Rose agreed. "You have to enjoy life while you can. That's what your Gram always said. Maybe you guys should reconsider the brew pub."

Maddie returned from the trash can, her phone held in the air. "Did you say brew pub? I don't think we have time for that. Marilyn just called. The crew of the show wants to check into the motel tomorrow."

CHAPTER THIRTY

*T*he cousins had just finished fussing over the finishing touches on the rooms when Marilyn and her crew arrived. They were an interesting bunch, who seemed to get along well.

Marilyn's assistant, Stacy, was as harried and chaotic as Marilyn was put-together and professional. She was friendly, with a halo of messy, honey-blond curls that bounced around her wide face as she talked. Even though she came off as a little disorganized, it was clear she knew how to run a contest.

Rob, the cameraman, was a bit introverted. Tall and slim, he barely said hello then hurried to his room. Maddie guessed he was the type who could easily become invisible at a party, but he clearly had a passion for photography, judging by the way he rushed out to take photos of the ocean as soon as he'd unpacked.

Kayleigh, who was responsible for making sure the pantry was stocked and all the ingredients were where they should be, was young but competent, even if she was a little dark in her clothing choices and makeup.

Two judges had checked in as well: Pia Turner, who Maddie knew from watching other cooking shows, and Alex Allen. They'd both been cordial and friendly, but took off to explore some new restaurant in Portland soon after checking in. The third judge, Hogan Fillery, was staying with relatives in the next town so he didn't need a room at the Beachcomber, which was a good thing since that would have meant that Maddie, Jules, and Gina would have had to squeeze into the storage room together. Maddie didn't think that would work out very well.

The crew for the baking show had gotten settled in their rooms, and everyone—except Robert, who was wandering around snapping pictures of the ocean from various angles—was sitting on the porch, enjoying a glass of lemonade that Gina had made from a mix that they'd found in the basket the welcome-wagon ladies had brought. Maddie was happy to see that the normal tension between Jules and Gina had disappeared. They weren't buddy-buddy, but at least it was progress.

"This is a great spot." Kayleigh gestured toward the ocean with her glass of lemonade. Her black nail polish contrasted with the pink swirling liquid as ice cubes clinked against the sides of the etched-glass vintage tumbler they'd found in the kitchen cupboard.

"Thanks. Our grandmother left it to us," Jules said from her perch on the railing.

Maddie said a silent prayer that there was no dry rot inside the railing, like there had been on the porch floorboards. Hopefully, Dex would have checked that out and mentioned it if he'd noticed.

This was nice, all the hard work behind them and just entertaining. She knew there would be more work as they tended to the needs of the guests over the week, but the good news was it was only a few days, so they wouldn't have to do any heavy cleaning until they left. Of course, that was also the bad news. Their income would be over once the guests did leave.

"Tell us about the contest." Gina leaned forward, holding her lemonade glass between her knees. "How does it work? Will you need to do a lot to the old donut shop building to set up?"

"Not too much. The kitchen is already configured perfectly, so it's mostly a matter of stocking ingredients," Stacy said.

"The ingredients get shipped in tomorrow, and we'll fill up the fridge and pantry," Kayleigh added.

"Then we just need to rearrange so we can put the camera equipment in the right places for Robert." Marilyn gestured toward the man squatting at the top of the stairs to snap a shot of a sailboat in the distance.

"And move those booths and tables so we can have a small audience. Which reminds me, you guys are invited to watch the taping."

"Thanks. So tomorrow you set up the venue, then the contest starts Monday, right?" Maddie asked.

Marilyn nodded. "That's right."

"When do the contestants arrive?" Jules asked.

"Tomorrow night," Marilyn said. "Don't expect them to be as chatty as we are. They mostly stay in their rooms and focus on the show. Besides, we start rehearsing at five a.m., then the taping starts at nine and goes until seven. That way we can get five days of competition into two days."

Gina frowned. "You do? I didn't realize that. On the TV show it's five days."

Stacy smiled. "We make it seem that way, but it's more cost-effective if we do the taping in two days. It's still the same competition, just with less time for sleeping in between eliminations."

"That makes sense." Jules stood. "Well, I'm going to wash out these glasses, and I'll put coffee in the lobby later on. Let us know if you need anything for your rooms."

CHAPTER THIRTY-ONE

"I think we're going to need a bigger washing machine." Jules was pulling wet towels out of the washing machine in the small laundry room next to the motel kitchen. She'd barely slept the night before, the full responsibility of running the motel finally hitting her.

"Lucky thing we don't have to do a room refresh every day." Maddie held her hand out for the next towel and shoved it into the dryer. Like most motels, they'd opted for room changes and fresh towels every third day instead of every day because it was better for the environment. It also saved them a lot of work.

"We're going to need to hire a cleaning crew," Gina said.

Jules glanced at her cousin, expecting a look of distaste on her face, but she merely looked pensive. Jules figured in her rich lifestyle, she wouldn't get her hands dirty with laundry, but while that might have been the case before, she got the impression maybe Gina didn't mind pitching in anymore.

"And get more towels." Maddie stuffed another one into the dryer. "I was also thinking we should get some beach towels and stock the rooms with them."

Gina leaned one shoulder against the wall and crossed her arms over her chest. "Now we'll really need a loan. Remember how they used to steal them at the Surfstone?"

Jules laughed. "Gram would get so mad. But she always said that it made a nice presentation to supply them in the rooms, so it was worth it."

Maddie put the last towel in and turned the dryer on. "We're going to need an influx of cash for all that. I wish we would get some word on that loan."

Jules felt the weight of her cousin's stare. "Nick said he was working on it, but we also need to find a way to capitalize on the momentum the baking contest will bring to Shell Cove. Getting the loan would be great, but let's not forget we have to repay it, and for that, we need a continuous flow of tourists."

"Good point. I think the current influx will last for a few weeks. The contest goes on TV next week, and that might bring even more people in. Ocean Brew was crammed this morning, and there were people milling around town, so word is already out." Gina had gone to

Ocean Brew to pick up coffees for the three of them that morning.

"That's great. At least there will be some sort of buzz about the town. We just need to figure out a way to keep it going."

"It looks like you'll have to work another miracle and come up with something as interesting as the *New England Baking Contest* to draw people in." Gina winked at Maddie.

Maddie snorted. "You make it sound so easy."

Ding!

The noise, which sounded like a very loud text message alert, came from the kitchen, but they all had their cell phones with them.

Gina pushed off from the wall and turned toward the kitchen. "That's the timer on the oven. I was experimenting with another pie."

CHAPTER THIRTY-TWO

*N*ick hadn't stayed long at the brew pub the previous night. The truth was he was a bit down at the way Jules had given him the cold shoulder. He knew he deserved it, but he'd felt a connection with her, even though they didn't know each other very well. He still wanted to explore that connection, but he had no idea how to make up for his idiotic behavior.

Even if Jules never spoke to him again, he still wanted the motel to get the loan. That had been more difficult than he'd expected without Gramps's stamp of approval. Even though there was no mortgage on the motel and it was seaside real estate, the bank saw no value in it, especially since there were no recent income statements, and prospects of income were grim, considering no one came to town. Or at least they hadn't until recently.

The town needed that motel if it was going to thrive, and just seeing what had happened in town over the past few days had Nick being hopeful about the future of Shell Cove. That was why he'd assured Gary that the bank itself would guarantee the loan. If the Beachcomber defaulted on it, the Shell Cove Bank and Trust would bear the responsibility.

Gramps would be mad about that, but Nick hadn't been able to find any other way to get Gary to consider it. It was still a long shot, but at least Gary was thinking it over, and Nick expected his response any time. Which was why he kept glancing at his phone as he gazed out the window, watching the activity about town from the front lobby of the bank.

"Expecting an important call?"

Gramps had come up behind him. Was it Nick's imagination, or did the old man have more of a spring in his step?

"Nah, just watching the town. It's really something how they've spruced it up. Isn't it?" His heart squeezed at the lie about the call. He hated lying to Gramps, but he wanted to get Gary's approval before he confessed what he'd been up to.

Gramps merely grunted, but Nick thought he saw a spark in his eye as he continued to gaze out at the street.

"More tourists is better for the bank too. Businesses will want to improve. New businesses will start up. They will need loans. People will have more money to invest and deposit into their savings accounts," Nick said.

That got a smile from his grandfather. "Now you're talking my language."

But Gramps's language hadn't always been about money. Nick remembered how Gramps used to laugh and enjoy life when Gram was alive. Even after, he'd had his friends to console him. Lately, he just sat alone in his office or at home. Nick didn't even think he had friends anymore. It was like Gramps had gotten broken, and Nick wished he knew how to fix him. Maybe a prosperous town would help.

"This baking contest is sure bringing people in. I know it's only temporary, but it's lit a fire under every business in town." Nick gestured to the window. "Look how happy everyone is. Maybe it will continue. I heard one of the girls from the Beachcomber talking about bringing more events to town. That will mean more money in the town coffers and eventually the banks. That should make you happy." Nick clapped his grandfather on the shoulder and headed back to his office.

THE TOWN COMING TO LIFE DID MAKE HENRY HAPPY. HE was just so used to being grumpy, he felt reluctant to let happiness back into his life. He had a lot to be grumpy for. Didn't he?

But as he sat on the bench at the end of the pier, drinking a coffee from Ocean Brew and watching the activity in the old donut shop, he wondered if he really did have a lot to be grumpy for. In some ways, his life had gone downhill when the town did. Part of that was that Rena had left. She had lit up his life, and even though she apparently didn't feel as strongly as he did, it had been hard with her just taking off and not even saying goodbye.

Decades had gone by, though. Why was he hanging onto that old wound? Had he just gotten so used to it, or was it that he didn't want to admit that he'd sat back and let his life and the town fade into gloom without doing anything about it?

"Excuse me, can I sit here? I need to tie my shoe." A middle-aged woman looked hopefully at the other end of the bench.

Henry shifted over. "Of course."

"Thanks." The woman sat and bent over, working at the lace of her sneaker. "Isn't it exciting? The baking contest, I mean. I've always wanted to see it."

"Yes, very." Henry really didn't think the contest itself was that exciting, but he had to admit the festive vibe around the pier was perking him up.

"I came to town to see it. I'm about an hour away, and I can't believe I've never heard of Shell Cove." The woman turned her head to look at him as she continued with the lace tying. "It's so quaint here!"

"It's a well-kept secret."

"I bet! Well, I'm not going to keep it a secret. In fact, I'm going to bring my family back on a vacation in the fall. Do you have any pumpkin contests or festivals?"

"Of course," Henry lied. He wasn't sure why, but he didn't want to discourage anyone from coming back to town. Plus, he had a sneaking suspicion that the town might actually have a pumpkin festival that fall, if some people had their way. His thoughts turned to Rena, Pearl, Leena, and Rose. They used to organize all sorts of things like that. It used to be fun.

"Great." The woman finished with her lace and stood. "Well, thanks for letting me share the bench. Have a great day."

The woman walked off, and Henry settled back with his coffee. His spirits were a little brighter. It was odd that just talking to a stranger had perked him up. He hadn't made the effort to talk to anyone, friend or stranger, in a long time. In his determination to wallow in self-pity, he'd denied himself the companionship of others, and he was starting to remember how nice that could be.

CHAPTER THIRTY-THREE

"*D*id Aggie check in yet?" Stacy poked her head into the kitchen, her gaze zeroing in on the pie plate on the table. "Who made pie?"

"I did." Gina suddenly felt self-conscious. Even though the apple pie had actually come out pretty good, it wasn't exactly aesthetically pleasing. She'd tried to cut leaves and flowers out of the dough like Gram used to, but it hadn't come out quite the same.

"Aggie's the only contestant that hasn't checked in yet," Maddie said.

The other four had checked in over the course of the evening and promptly disappeared into their rooms, just like Marilyn had said they would.

"Hmm. That's a bit worrisome. She's almost eighty, and her son said he hadn't heard from her." Stacy glanced out the window. "It's dark out, and she can't see well at night."

"I hope she didn't get lost." Maddie's voice was laced with genuine concern.

"Me too." Stacy chewed her bottom lip. "I'm not sure what to do, though. Maybe she's just taking her time. He said she drives slow and she hates being checked up on."

Jules nodded. "She'll probably show up any minute."

Stacy kept eyeing the pie, and Gina didn't want to be rude. "Would you like a piece?"

"I thought you'd never ask." Stacy plopped down at the table, and Gina served her a piece on one of Gram's pink etched-depression-glass dessert dishes.

Butterflies flapped in Gina's stomach as Stacy took a bite. Her cousins had said the pie was good earlier, but they were probably just being polite. Stacy was in a pie baking contest. She had experience, and she wasn't related to Gina, so she didn't have to be nice.

"Yumm. This is really good." Stacy loaded up her fork.

"Thanks. I used to make pies with my grandmother, who owned this motel," Gina said.

Stacy looked around the kitchen. "How interesting. That might be a nice interest piece for the show." Stacy pointed her fork at Gina. "You should be in the contest."

Gina panicked. "Very funny. I'm sure my pie isn't anything like the gourmet concoctions your contestants will make."

Stacy raised her brow. "Don't be too sure. Lucky for you, we already have our contestants. We can't deviate from the program now."

As Gina watched Stacy gobble up the pie, she realized she felt happy and less stressed than she had in a long time. The last year with Hugh had been challenging. But right then, she couldn't care less about her husband. Good riddance to him. And the desire to return to her old life in Boston was fading.

CHAPTER THIRTY-FOUR

"Isn't it wonderful to see the town bustling with action again?" Rose was sitting with Pearl and Leena at one of the cafe tables that Cassie had put on the brick patio outside Ocean Brew. It was just dusk, and the sky was painted in hues of pink and turquoise. A warm sea breeze stirred the air, and the quaint Main Street, with its antique storefronts and fairy lights and the Atlantic Ocean beyond, had a magical feel.

"Sure is." Leena broke off a piece of her chocolate brownie. "The town looks better than it has in ages. I wish we could get those empty stores to open up, though."

"Me too. Remember when the wine and cheese shop was over there?" Pearl pointed to a vacant storefront. "It used to be so much fun to go to the wine tastings."

"And the bookstore across the street." Pearl sighed and pinched a crumb from the chocolate chip cookie she had on a napkin in front of her then popped it into her mouth. "We need a good bookstore again. People love to read at the beach."

"And what about the piano bar! Remember how we used to sing the night away over martinis?" Leena's lips tugged in a smile, a faraway look on her face.

"Maybe we can get back to that." Rose finished off her muffin as she watched the people milling about. There were plenty of tourists with their colorful shorts and casual sandals. They were browsing in the shops, eating ice cream, and best of all, laughing and having a good time.

"I think this can work. The town can come back. Everyone looks so happy," Pearl said.

"Even Henry Barlowe must be caught up in the festive mood. I saw him chatting with a tourist earlier today," Leena said.

Rose turned to her. "Really? Huh, will miracles never cease? I thought he was too old to change his crotchety ways. I never really understood why he got so sour."

"Me either." Pearl pinched off another crumb of muffin. "I know it had to do with Rena leaving. She said he never even acknowledged her goodbye letter! She was very hurt."

Rose frowned. "Then why is he acting like the one who got hurt?"

Leena shrugged. "Men! Who can figure them out?"

"No one." Pearl glanced over at the pier, where the baking show crew was still busy inside the old donut shop. "The baking show has brought tourists to town, and that's a good thing, but we need to figure out ways to keep those tourists coming."

"That's why we need Maddie to take the chamber of commerce position," Rose said. "Her positive attitude is what this town needs. And we went to great lengths to convince Mayor Martindale to make that position available again."

Tourism drying up in Shell Cove had had a domino effect. Businesses closed. The town took in less money in taxes and fees and eventually had no money to promote tourism. Any town jobs that had been related to that, and even some that hadn't been related, had been eliminated.

"Lucky thing there's money in the coffers now from the permit fees for the baking contest," Leena said.

Pearl's blue eyes gleamed with mischief as she took a five-dollar bill out of her purse. "How much do you want to bet that Maddie has this town back on its feet by the end of summer?"

Leena glanced at the money and shook her head.

"No one wants to bet against that. We don't want to jinx it. But it does look like I'm going to clean up on the Jules and Nick bet if the way she was acting at the ice cream parlor the other night is any indication."

"Don't count them out yet." Rose looked smug. "You know how I usually win these bets. I'm a good judge of character. And I'm pretty sure I'm going to win the bet about the girls staying. At first I wasn't sure about Gina, but now I think the town is growing on her."

"She does seem interested in Rena's pies," Pearl pointed out.

Leena scowled. "It's too soon to tell. She sold her car, and I still say she's going to bolt."

"Maybe, maybe not." Rose's gaze was now fixed on the Saltwater Sweets shop. "I'll give you a chance to make some of your money back. I bet Deena will be remarried within the year."

"What?" Leena jerked her head toward the store. "To her new guy?"

Through the window, they could see Deena beaming up at the tall man who they assumed was her new flame.

"Jeepers, it looks like they have it bad. But there's always a honeymoon phase when couples first meet. Some people act a lot nicer than they really are at first," Leena said knowingly. "I'll take that bet. I hate to wish a breakup on Deena, and I hope it works out, but the odds are against it."

"I heard he has a lot of money," Pearl said.

"Even more reason to be suspicious of him," Leena replied.

Pearl batted at her friend's arm. "Oh, Leena, you're always so skeptical. Everything is going to work out great for everyone. You'll see."

CHAPTER THIRTY-FIVE

Gina tucked her feet under herself on the porch rocker and balanced the dessert plate in her lap. Closing her eyes, she took a bite of pie. It was pretty good, if she did say so herself. Sure the presentation wasn't exactly magazine-worthy, but she could work on that. Besides, she wouldn't be serving the pie to anyone who cared what it looked like.

For the first time in a long time, she felt a glow of pride. It was so different from her previous life and better in a lot of ways. Not just the part about running the motel and being away from the stress and constant demeaning jabs of working with Hugh. The scenery here was a lot nicer than the city. The sound of the waves and the stars above trumped smog and city traffic any day, as far as Gina was concerned.

She'd been skeptical about Shell Cove at first, but

she had to admit that the town had possibilities. Could there be a place for her in its community? Her relationship with Jules had improved, and she was actually enjoying the bond that was forming with her two cousins. They were practically the only family she had, and she was pretty sure they would both be staying in Shell Cove.

"It's pretty out here at night. Isn't it?" Maddie stood in the doorway, a steaming hot chocolate in her hand. "Mind if I join you?"

"Not at all." Gina was surprised to discover she would actually enjoy the company.

"I knew things were all going to work out," Maddie said. "Well, I mean, I know they haven't totally worked out yet, but look how far we've come. The phone has been ringing all day with people wanting a room. Too bad we don't have more to rent. But this proves the town can be revived and the motel will do well. We just need to get more people here."

Gina smiled, thinking of the old avocado rotary dial phone ringing in the kitchen. "Yeah, but how?"

"Hey, you guys." Jules came out the door and sat on one of the chairs. "I thought I heard voices out here."

Maddie's face creased in concern. "Were we being too loud? I don't want to wake the guests."

"No. I don't think they can hear you over there. I was in the lobby making sure things are set up for tomorrow morning," Jules said. "I put Mr. Coffee out there so people can pour their own."

"Oh, hi." Marilyn came around the corner of the motel. "Thought I heard voices. Did Aggie check in? She's in room ten, right? She's not answering her door."

Maddie looked concerned. "No, I thought she might have called you to say she'd been delayed."

Marilyn pulled her phone out of the pocket of her long cardigan. "Nope. This might be a problem."

"Maybe she'll show up any minute." Jules looked toward the road, as if expecting to see headlights.

"I don't think so. It's almost ten o'clock. She wouldn't be up this late, especially with an early start tomorrow," Marilyn said.

"That is worrisome." Gina felt a pang of concern for the older woman, even though she didn't know her.

"Did you find her?" Stacy appeared from the other side of the motel. Apparently they'd been scouring the premises for poor Aggie.

Marilyn sighed and flopped into a chair. "No. This isn't good, not good at all."

"Well, maybe she had to stop at another motel because it got dark. Did you talk to her son?" Maddie asked. "I'm sure she's okay, or we would have heard."

"He doesn't answer," Marilyn said. "But it's not just if she's okay. I mean, I hope she is, but it's the contest. Even if she shows up later, she might not be up to competing early in the morning."

229

"You said you have practice then. Maybe she could miss some of that," Jules suggested.

"No. It doesn't work that way. She'd have to be there, or she won't know where to stand while filming," Stacy said.

"Oh, well, maybe she'll have to forfeit or something."

"No can do. We have to have five contestants." Stacy glanced at Marilyn. "Should we call corporate and tell them it's off?"

Maddie jumped to her feet. "Off? What do you mean?"

"We can't have the contest without five contestants. Everything is geared for five—the stations, the judging, the food, everything. The way the eliminations work depends on five, otherwise the whole timing of the production will be off."

Maddie looked from Stacy to Marilyn. "So you just pack up and leave? What about all the people that have come to town to see it? What will you air on the TV show next week?"

"It stinks to have to disappoint them, and we'd have to air an old episode. But we don't have much choice."

Gina's heart sank. If they canceled the contest, that wouldn't be good for Shell Cove. The tourists would go home with a bad taste in their mouths, and she knew Maddie was counting on the television show to bring more people to town when it aired. There had to be a solution. She forked up another piece of pie, her fork clinking on the plate.

Everyone's gaze fell on the plate then drifted up to Gina's face.

"Unless we had another person who could make pies to take her place in the contest," Stacy said.

"What? No. You don't mean me?" Gina felt a flutter of panic.

"It was good pie," Stacy said.

"Yeah, but I'm not a professional baker." Gina gestured toward the plate. "It doesn't even look good." Surely Stacy couldn't be serious. The hopeful look on her cousins' faces gave Gina pause. If the contest was called off, all their hard work might be for nothing. They were counting on her. Could she take Aggie's place in the contest?

"You don't have to be a professional." Stacy turned to Marilyn. "It would be a great human-interest angle. Local baker competes in contest. What do you think? We have time to work it into some segments."

"It could work," Marilyn said. "It's about the only option we have right now."

"She still has time to show up, right?" Gina hoped that Aggie was okay and just stopping on her route when it took too long to drive there and became dark. "I'd just be a stand-in."

"She could. I hope she will," Stacy said. "But we

can't guarantee she will. And if she doesn't, you need to be ready to compete."

Gina took a deep breath. Everyone was looking at her with hopeful eyes. No one had depended on her before. In fact, Hugh had had her convinced she was rather useless. She felt empowered and a little excited to compete with her pie. What was the harm? She would probably get eliminated in the first contest anyway.

"Okay, I'll do it."

CHAPTER THIRTY-SIX

The more Gina thought about the contest, the more she realized she wanted to win, not just to fill up a space but to really put her best foot forward. But she needed an edge over the other competitors. They were all a lot more experienced than she was. She needed Gram's recipes the welcome-wagon ladies had raved about.

"Cousin Tina didn't find anything? Not even some old index cards with recipes scribbled on them?" Gina asked Jules.

"Nothing. I messaged her three times and called. She's cleaned out most of the house, but I made her look in every cupboard."

"There are some good recipes on the internet." Maddie was sitting at the kitchen table, hunched over her laptop, typing furiously. "How about an Ina Garten one? Oh wait! Paula Deen. She's popular. We'll need more butter though."

Gina wasn't encouraged. "It seems like those are recipes anyone could use. We need something special. Something unique. I'm sure Gram wouldn't have thrown hers out. They must be stored somewhere."

Maddie looked up at Gina. "Wait a minute. Stored. What if they are right here in that storage area?"

"Of course! I saw some boxes in there that looked more personal." Gina was out the door and on her way to the storage area before the last word left her lips.

"I THINK I MIGHT HAVE FOUND SOMETHING." MADDIE watched as Gina pulled a long, narrow wooden box out of the storage container she'd been foraging through. They were sitting on Gina's bed in the storage area, the contents of the boxes strewn about the floor.

Maddie had been starting to lose hope and was ready to suggest just going with one of the recipes from the internet, but she could sense that Gina really wanted recipes that were special. Maybe it was because it gave her a connection to Gram, or maybe it was because she really wanted to win. She wasn't sure which, but it was welcome because she was seeing a passion in Gina that had been missing for a long time.

And something else had changed too. Jules was looking just as hard as Gina for the recipes. They weren't bickering or giving each other the cold shoulder.

Gina opened the box. "This could be it."

She turned the box to face them. The front half of the box had index cards lined up like an index file in a library. The back half had papers and magazine clippings stacked on top of each other. Maddie's quick glance told her they were, indeed, recipes.

Jules picked out one of the cards. "This is for Gram's sour cream coffee cake. I used to love that."

Maddie's eyes misted as she recognized Gram's writing, and childhood memories of Gram's delicious coffee cake bubbled up.

"We need to find the pie recipes." Gina carefully took a stack of cards out, and they started sorting through them.

"Here's one for that cinnamon crust Pearl mentioned at the town meeting." Jules lay a yellowed, food-stained card aside.

"And here's one for an apple pie with sour cream. That sounds good." Maddie laid it next to the cinnamon crust. "I suppose they have specific types of pies you have to make for the contest."

"And probably ingredient challenges, where you have to work with what they give you," Jules said.

Gina took a deep breath, uncertainty darkening her

expression. "Right. Maybe I'm not experienced enough for this."

"No, no." Maddie touched her arm. "You'll be fine. What's the worst thing that could happen?"

Gina laughed. "Good point. It will be a miracle if I make it past the first elimination, anyway, so I'll probably only need to make one pie. But it still might be smart to study these recipes."

Gina pulled the magazine clippings and other papers out of the back and started to search through them. She stopped at one that looked like an envelope. "What's this?"

The front of the envelope had a name and address on it. Henry Barlowe.

"Wait, is that for Henry down at the bank?" Maddie reached for it.

"The welcome-wagon ladies did say he and Gram used to be friends."

"It's sealed." Maddie picked at the edge of the flap, but the old glue held tight. "I guess she never gave it to him. No postmark or anything."

"That's odd. It seems like she meant to." Gina riffled through the rest of the papers that had been in the box. "Maybe it got lost in the stack of paperwork, and she never got a chance."

"Should we give it to him?" Maddie asked.

"I guess we can ask Pearl, Rose, and Leena," Jules said. "It seems like he should have it."

"I agree." Maddie stood with the letter in hand. "I'll put it in the kitchen. If we're done here, I think I should get to bed. We need our rest for tomorrow, and Gina probably needs some time to concentrate." She reached across the bed to hug her cousin. "Don't stay up too late."

Jules stood too. "We'll help you clean this up tomorrow." Then she did something that surprised Maddie. She hugged Gina too.

Maddie started toward the kitchen, a smile tugging the corners of her lips. It looked like Gina and Jules had finally gotten past their issues. She could almost feel Gram's approval radiating through the motel.

CHAPTER THIRTY-SEVEN

The old donut shop was abuzz with activity the following morning. Tourists packed the pier and spilled out into the town. The merchants could be seen smiling in their shops as customers left with bulging shopping bags. Cassie had added several new tables on the patio to take advantage of the swell of traffic.

Maddie and Jules walked Gina to the old donut shop.

"You got this." Maddie held up her fist.

"Don't be nervous. Remember this is for fun." Jules held hers up, too, and the three of them fist-bumped.

"And the prize money." Rose appeared at Jules's elbow.

"Prize money? I didn't even think about that." Maddie thought about all the expenses that were adding up at the motel. "I don't even know how much it is."

"Ten thousand dollars," Leena said. "That could help the motel."

"It sure could. Especially since there hasn't been any word on the loan," Jules said then apparently seeing the look of panic on her cousin's face, she hastened to add, "But don't worry about that, Gina. Just do your best. Even getting in there and doing this is a win."

Gina smiled then took a deep breath. "Well, I better go inside."

"Good luck in there," Rose said.

"Thanks."

"Don't worry," Pearl said. "Your grandmother is watching over you."

"Break a leg!" Leena shouted awkwardly as Gina headed toward the door of the old donut shop.

"Well, this is so exciting." Rose clapped her hands and craned to look in the window of the shop, where they could see the crew bustling around to get things ready.

"And what a beautiful day for it!" Maddie leaned over the railing and looked down at the foamy edge of the surf below the pier. Her gaze traveled to the long stretch of beach. The sugar-white sand went on as far as the eye could see on both sides. On one side of the pier, she could see the cliff of rocks that was next to the Beachcomber. The other side was mostly just dunes.

Something partially hidden by the dunes caught her eye. She'd never looked closely at that section of the beach before. She'd been so busy with the motel that she hadn't had much time to spend on the beach at all. But something about the cottage struck her fancy and made her want to investigate further.

She shaded her eyes and squinted, trying to get a better look. She could only see a part of it: a weathered roof, peeling paint, and shutters with starfish cutouts. It looked old and was in need of work, but the look of it and the location charmed her.

"What's that?" She pointed toward the house.

"That's Starfish Cottage," Leena said. "It's been empty for a while."

"Why?"

"The owner used to rent it for vacations, but when the tourists stopped coming, there was no one to rent it," Rose said.

"It's old." Pearl looked wistful. "I seem to recall my mother saying there was some sort of mystery surrounding the original owner."

A mystery? How intriguing. Maddie couldn't take her eyes off the cottage. She could picture herself sitting on the porch. If she stayed in town, she would need a place to live. She couldn't stay at the motel forever, and she'd always dreamed of a cottage on the beach.

"I wonder if they'd sell it. Real estate in town must

be pretty cheap right about now." Not that she had any money to buy it.

"I think the bank might own it," Rose said. "Unfortunately, a lot of people defaulted on their mortgages, and the bank has a surplus. Henry might be willing to make a deal."

"Oh! Speaking of the bank, I found this letter." Maddie pulled the letter they'd found in Gram's recipes out of her pocket.

"For Henry? Why did she never send it?" Rose asked.

"I have no idea. It was in with some old recipes, and we think maybe it got lost in the shuffle somehow," Maddie said.

"Well, what do you know?" Rose scanned the crowd. "I think we should make it a point to see that he gets it."

JULES STAYED BEHIND WHEN THE WELCOME-WAGON ladies went off to find Henry, and Maddie ran up to Ocean Brew for coffees. She had a task of her own. She'd spotted Nick in the crowd and wanted to seek him out. She was feeling guilty about the way she'd acted toward him. She was still put off by the whole thing about the inspection, but maybe she should let past grievances lie.

Nick saw her coming toward him. His expression turned hopeful and a little wary, as if he were expecting her to yell at him again. She couldn't blame him after the way she'd acted on the park bench.

"Hi. I can't believe all the people that turned out for this. I heard one of your cousins is competing in it." Nick gave Jules an inquisitive look, as if wondering how that had happened.

"One of the contestants didn't show up, so Gina got roped into taking her place," Jules said. "I think she's secretly kind of excited."

Nick laughed. "Well, I hope she wins."

"I doubt she aspires to that, but if she didn't agree to compete, then they would have had to call off the contest, so it's good for all of us."

"It sure is. I haven't seen the town this busy since I was a kid." Nick smiled down at her, and Jules's heart fluttered. His eyes were kind and a little regretful.

She'd felt a connection at the coffee shop that day, but had she ruined it? Should she apologize? He was the one who messed up, but he had apologized for that. Not knowing what to say, she turned to a more general topic. "The motel is fully booked. Of course it's mostly the crew for the show, but we've been getting calls from people who want to stay with us. We've even booked a few for next week."

"Really? That's great. Maybe there's hope for this

town after all." Nick looked as if he were going to say more.

Jules figured that would be a good time to apologize and try to start over. "Look, I—"

Ding!

The ping of Nick's phone stole his attention. He looked at the display then cast her an apologetic glance. "I have to get this."

"Of course," she said, but he was already turning away, the phone to his ear.

So much for apologizing and getting a second chance to continue on their path to becoming friends.

"GOOD NEWS." GARY'S VOICE ON THE OTHER END OF the line lifted Nick's spirits even further. Not only was Jules being less hostile, but his hope that the loan for the Beachcomber would be approved might actually come true.

"You approved the loan?" Nick asked.

"Yes. The independent appraisal came back, and we'll take the chance, especially with your branch's guarantee."

"That's great news! Thanks so much for considering this." Nick glanced around and lowered his voice. "I'd appreciate it if you didn't mention this to my grandfather just yet."

"As you wish." Gary hung up, and Nick turned to give Jules the good news. His heart fell when the space she'd been standing in was empty. He scanned the crowd, looking for her dark curls, but she was nowhere to be found.

Maybe she didn't want to make up with him after all.

Nick put the phone in his pocket and headed into the crowd. It was time to come clean with his grandfather and hope he hadn't ruined that relationship too.

CHAPTER THIRTY-EIGHT

"*A*ndy Sugarman... I'm sorry, but you're eliminated." Hogan Fillery looked at the pastry chef from his perch behind the judging table, his dark eyes filled with sympathy. "Please pack your rolling pin and go."

Gina let out her breath and practically fainted. She'd made it through the first round? It was just dumb luck. Andy had burned the edges of his pie crust, and that mistake had gotten him eliminated.

Gina looked down at the mint cream Oreo cookie crust pie she'd plated. It sat on the white plate, a sprig of mint and two cookies on the side. It looked pretty good. Studying plating techniques online all night had paid off.

"Congratulations!" Maddie rushed up to give her a hug.

"Thanks. I lucked out." Gina tried to play it off, but she was proud of her work. Still, she knew she'd gotten lucky and cautioned herself not to get too cocky about it. The second competition would start in an hour, and that one would likely be her last.

She glanced around the room. Kayleigh was busy rearranging things in the fridge and on the pantry shelves. The other contestants, Brad, Sonja, and Bronwyn, were in their areas setting up. Gina had been surprised that everyone kept to themselves. There was no chatting or making friends with the other contestants. Apparently it was better not to get too attached since only one person could win.

Stacy had set up a long table for the judges to sit at. They were all still there. Someone must have brought them coffees from Ocean Brew. Gina recognized the Styrofoam cups with the wave logo in front of them. They chatted and laughed among themselves.

"I better get my things ready." Gina glanced over at the other contestants again. She actually wasn't sure what to do to get ready, but they all looked pretty serious about it. "Hey, did Aggie ever check in?"

Maddie's smile faded. "No. I haven't checked with Marilyn to see if she's heard from her, but I'm keeping the room open for her. Speaking of which, I guess poor Andy will be checking out today. I better go clean his room out and call back some people who wanted to make a reservation."

Maddie said goodbye to her cousin and hurried to her car in the town parking lot near the pier. She wanted to get back before the second contest started so she could be there to support Gina.

She'd watched the first round with butterflies in her stomach as Gina had rushed around assembling ingredients for the pie. How she knew what to grab was beyond Maddie. Apparently staying up all night to study Gram's recipes had paid off for the contest.

Gina's pie looked pretty good, too, much better than her previous attempts at the motel. Maddie had watched the expressions on the judges' faces when they'd taken a taste, and she was sure they'd all liked it. She knew Gina was still there only because of Andy's mistake, but she was keeping her fingers crossed for her cousin to survive the next round.

She hopped in her car in the parking lot and glanced once at Starfish Cottage before driving off to the motel.

CHAPTER THIRTY-NINE

*H*enry sat down on the bench at the end of the pier and stared at the envelope in his hand. His eyes misted at the familiar handwriting, Rena's handwriting.

He glanced up at Rose, whose expression bore a mixture of curiosity and sympathy.

"Where did you get this?" he asked.

"The girls found it stored away in a box of recipes in the storage room at the Beachcomber."

"But why do you think Rena would have done that?" Henry's gaze flicked from Rose to Pearl to Leena. It didn't make much sense to write a letter to him then put it in a box for thirty years. But these women knew Rena best. Maybe they knew something he didn't.

"Henry, I think she meant to give it to you, but something must have happened," Pearl said.

"Got on, open it." Leena gestured to the letter impatiently.

Henry was nervous. He wasn't even sure he wanted to know what was in the letter. But his three old friends were watching, so he turned the envelope over and ran his finger under the flap. Inside was a piece of white paper with more of Rena's handwriting.

Dear Henry,

I'm writing this down because I'm afraid I won't be able to come up with the right words in person. As you know, the drop in tourist trade has caused the Beachcomber to become a loss. Because of that, my time in Shell Cove is short.

But I didn't want to leave without letting you know how much you have meant to me over these years. When Donald died, I thought I would never find another as charming, but you, dear Henry, have managed to capture my heart.

I know nothing more than friendship has come of it. I was good friends with your wife and you with Don, so the memories of our past get in the way. But I hope in time our friendship could grow.

Even though I am leaving, I will not be too far. I'm going to focus my time in Seal Harbor, where I have another motel that needs my attention now.

Maybe you could come to visit?

I know you have your life and business here, but just because

I'm leaving doesn't mean we have to say goodbye. Seal Harbor is only an hour away.

I know I'm a coward to mail this to you instead of giving it in person, but if I am wrong about our friendship, then I couldn't bear for you to have the discomfort of having to tell me to my face.

I will still be at the motel until the twelfth and await your answer.

Yours,

Rena

HENRY STARED AT THE LETTER FOR A LONG TIME. IT had all been a stupid misunderstanding? Henry looked up at his friends. "I thought she didn't care. I always thought she just left without even saying goodbye to me, like our friendship meant nothing to her."

Pearl shook her head. "It didn't mean nothing. I've tried to tell you over the years, but you're too stubborn to listen."

Henry turned the envelope over. "But she never mailed it."

"Packing up the motel was hectic for her. We think she meant to, but the letter got shuffled in with other papers, and she thought she'd put it in the motel mailbox for the postman to collect," Rose said.

"She mentioned her disappointment that you never said anything about the letter quite a few times," Pearl added.

"That's why she never came back here. We always went to visit her," Leena said.

"And I thought it was because she didn't want to see me." Henry looked out at the ocean and felt the years fall away. What a waste. He'd held on to a grudge that wasn't even real. He'd been a stubborn fool, and that had caused him to miss out. He wasn't going to waste any more time on nursing old grudges. He didn't know how many years he had left, but he wanted to make them count.

He smiled at Rose, Pearl, and Leena. "Thank you so much for bringing this to me. I apologize for being so cranky all these years. I'll do better. I promise."

"That's the spirit, Henry!" Pearl hugged him, and it felt awkward, but only for a few seconds.

"We've missed you, Henry," Rose smiled at him then clapped her hands and turned to the others. "Okay, ladies, let's get a move on. The second round of the contest is about to start, and I want a good seat."

Henry smiled as he watched the three ladies walk off. They'd been good friends once, long ago, and he wanted to see if he could get back to that. It seemed like they wanted that too.

"Gramps, are you okay?"

"Never better, my boy!" Henry's smile faded a notch at the look of angst on Nick's face. "What's going on?"

"Well, I have something to tell you, and I don't want you to be mad at me."

"Mad?" Henry couldn't imagine why Nick thought he would ever be mad at him. He doted on the boy. Didn't he? Or had his grumpy demeanor over the past few decades come off as anger? "I could never be mad at you. What is it?"

"It has to do with the bank, Gramps." Nick hesitated, as if trying to find the right words.

"Okay." Henry smiled to encourage him.

Nick took a deep breath. "It's about the loan for the Beachcomber."

Henry's cheeks flushed with shame, remembering how he'd told Nick that they couldn't give Jules the loan. He'd done that out of bitterness because of the way he'd thought things had ended with Rena. He needed to make that right. "I don't think—"

Nick held up his hand, stopping Henry midsentence. "I know you don't think it's a good investment for the bank, but I disagree. And it's not just about the bank. It's about the town. Look how the town has come back to life." Nick gestured toward the street brimming with tourists. "The town needs a motel, and I think Jules and her cousins can revive the Beachcomber, but they're going to need our help."

"Yes, you're right." Henry wondered if Nick had heard him, because Nick hurried to continue justifying his actions.

"I don't like to disagree with you or go behind your

back, but I felt I had no choice. I had to do what I knew was right in my heart. You taught me that."

"You went behind my back?" Henry could tell that Nick was expecting him to be mad, but it was the opposite. He was proud. Nick had taken a stand.

"Yes. I went to Gary to see if I could get the loan pushed through."

"Why?"

"You'd made it clear that you weren't going to approve it. I want this town to grow, and giving a loan to the Beachcomber so it can attract tourists is part of it." Nick's expression softened. "I hope you won't be mad at me, Gramps. I love you, but on this one, you were just plain wrong."

Henry and Nick stared at each other for a few seconds. Then Henry burst into laughter and clapped his grandson on the back. "I couldn't agree more. You did good."

"Huh?" Nick looked completely confused.

Henry sighed. "I was a fool and let my old feelings get in the way. You did the right thing. How did you do it? It must have been hard with no earnings statements since the motel has been closed."

Nick's expression turned sheepish. "I guaranteed the loan from our branch."

"Oh, good idea."

"You're not mad that our branch guaranteed the loan?" Nick seemed doubtful.

"No, I have every confidence the Beachcomber will thrive and the loan will be repaid fully. And you're right. This town needs a good motel if it's going to make a comeback." Henry looked around again at the crowds. "And I do believe it will make a comeback. Come on. Let's go get a beer… I feel like celebrating. You and I and this town are in for great things."

CHAPTER FORTY

"I'm so excited that you're still in the contest!" Maddie slipped her arm around Gina's shoulder and gave her a squeeze as they watched Sonja Childs loading up her car in the parking lot of the Beachcomber. Sonja had been eliminated for lack of creativity.

"It doesn't seem fair," Gina said. "She knows what she's doing, and I don't."

Judging by the way Sonja was slamming things into her trunk and glaring over at Gina, she didn't think it was fair either.

"Maybe that's why you beat her. Sometimes when you've been doing something for a while, you get so bogged down in knowing what you are supposed to do that you lose that creative spark," Jules said.

Gina shrugged. "I'm sure it was just a fluke, but it's kind of fun to still be in the contest."

"I'm glad you stayed, and she got cut." They turned to see another of the contestants, Bronwyn Saunders, approaching. Apparently she'd been walking on the beach. She had her sandals in one hand and a huge shell in the other. "I know it sounds mean, but she's not a nice person. I've competed against her before."

Maddie wasn't sure what to say about that. She preferred to be positive, so she decided to compliment Bronwyn. "I thought your pie was very pretty with the whipped cream sculpture on top."

Bronwyn laughed. "Kept me in the contest, I guess. But Gina's was the best with those molded dough flowers and leaves. Where did you learn that? Did you go to a fancy pastry school?"

Gina laughed. "No, my grandmother taught me when I was a kid. I haven't actually even done much with pie in years, but I guess I got lucky today."

"I learned from my grandmother too! In fact, that's why I'm here. She sacrificed so much to teach me and put me through pastry school, and now..." Bronwyn's voice trailed off, and she looked down at the shell in her hand. "She's sick."

Maddie felt a surge of sympathy for the girl. Her short blond hair, cornflower-blue eyes, and sprinkling of freckles across her nose made her look like she couldn't be more than twenty-five. Too young to have to deal with a sick grandmother. "I'm so sorry."

Bronwyn gave her a small smile. "Thanks. I want to take her to a cancer clinic in Mexico, but that costs money."

"You want to use the contest money," Jules said.

Maddie hadn't given much thought to the prize money because she hadn't expected Gina to make it that far. They could use it for the motel—she knew because she'd run the numbers last night, and they would run out of money soon, even with the increase in bookings. She hadn't told her cousins yet. She didn't want to spoil things when it finally seemed like everything was going well. But even though the motel could use the money, she found herself hoping that Bronwyn won the contest.

"It will be hard to beat Brad. He's pretty good and a lot more experienced. His wife is going to have a baby soon." Bronwyn turned to Gina with a smile. "And it's apparently hard to beat you too."

Brad Rutledge, the third remaining contestant, was a chef at a fancy restaurant in Miami. He was in his midfifties, which Maddie supposed afforded him several decades of experience over Bronwyn.

"You never know. Sometimes experience isn't everything." Maddie wanted to encourage Bronwyn.

"True, and on that note, I'd better get to my room,"

Bronwyn said as Sonja sped out of the lot. "I need to be well rested for the contest. Good luck tomorrow."

"She seems nice," Jules said.

"She does. And now that Sonja is gone, we have an open room. Do you want it, Gina?" Maddie asked.

Gina mulled it over for a few seconds. "Nah, I'm kind of starting to like the storage room, and besides, I don't want to get into moving until the contest is over."

Jules sighed. "I guess we'll have plenty of rooms open then."

"You'd be surprised." Maddie oozed optimism. "We have two reservations for a few days following the contest and one for the week after. Which brings up the question, What will we do if the motel gets full again? We don't want to take up too many of the rooms."

"What did Gram do?" Jules asked. "I don't remember her actually living at any of the motels."

"She didn't. She hired help to man the front desk at night, then it was closed after a certain time. Keys left in envelopes under the planter for late check-ins. At least that's what Rose told me. Gram lived in that little Victorian on the end of Grove Street here in town."

"The one with the fancy trim work?" Jules asked.

"Yep." Maddie thought about Starfish Cottage. Did she dare to hope? "If we decide to stay in town and make a go of this long-term, we can't very well live at the motel."

"Yeah, one-room living gets tedious," Jules said.

"But that begs the question: Are we staying here for the long-term?"

"Gram's will didn't specify a time frame, just that we had to try to make a go of it, and I think this place has potential." Maddie buried thoughts about the accounting spreadsheet. She wanted it to work out, and they were just getting started. Of course they wouldn't show a profit right away.

"It is, but we need more time. The baking show has been great for bringing tourists in, but we don't know if we can sustain that long-term. For now, it makes sense to take it day by day." Jules looked out at the ocean. "But I have to say, I am getting pretty attached to this place. I wouldn't mind staying."

"Me too." Maddie glanced at Gina. She'd been silent for the last part of the conversation, and Maddie hoped that her cousin would chime in about whether she intended to stay in Shell Cove or go back to her fancy lifestyle in Boston.

But instead of saying anything on the topic, Gina yawned. "Well, I guess I'll turn in. Tomorrow's a big day, and I need my beauty rest."

CHAPTER FORTY-ONE

The next day, Jules went with Maddie to the pier. Gina had left earlier and was already inside going over the day's schedule with Marilyn and the rest of the crew and contestants.

"Do you think she has a chance?" Maddie asked.

"I don't know, but either way, it's an accomplishment that she's come this far." Jules glanced in the window.

They'd sectioned off the big kitchen area into individual spots, and Gina was at hers lining up ingredients, which Jules assumed, were for the first contest. "She's changed. At first, I thought she seemed standoffish, but she's really warmed up over the past few days."

Maddie nodded. "She has. I thought she was going to bug out of the motel project, but now I think she is getting into it."

Jules scanned the crowd, looking for Nick, but didn't see him. It was just as well. It was clear they weren't going to be friends. There were plenty of other friends for her in Shell Cove, she thought as Rose, Leena, and Pearl approached them.

"This is so exciting, isn't it?" Rose asked.

"It sure is. Look at all the people! It's like the good old days," Pearl gushed.

"It's great to see you. Almost everyone from town is here, even Deena and her new man." Leena waved to the couple, who started over.

"Hi, girls. It's good to see you. Have you met Chuck?" Deena gestured toward the man. He was tall with kind brown eyes, slightly balding, but had a pleasant demeanor.

Introductions were made all around. The entire time, Deena beamed up at Chuck. They made a cute couple. Deena was about a foot shorter than Chuck, and her soft brown eyes and honey-blond bob made her look a lot younger than she probably was.

Chuck patted her hand and beamed back. Clearly they were in love. Jules felt a pang of… regret? Her last relationship had been several years ago, and she hadn't met anyone that she wanted to get serious about since— except maybe Nick. She brushed thoughts of him away. She barely knew the guy, and it was best not to wonder about what might have been.

"Well, we better get back to Saltwater Sweets. We just came down to check things out. We're making sea salted caramels today."

Jules's mouth watered as Deena and Chuck bid their goodbyes.

"It's time!" Pearl shoved her phone back into her purse. "Let's head inside."

THE DAY WENT BY FASTER THAN GINA COULD HAVE EVER imagined. By some miracle, she made it through the first round. Brad got eliminated, probably because he couldn't concentrate. His wife called at the beginning of the contest to tell him she thought she might be in labor. He'd wanted to just forfeit and rush off, but the wife begged him to at least finish one round since the doctor had told her it could be false labor or could take hours.

That had worked in Gina and Bronwyn's favor, and the two of them stood in front of the judges for the final elimination. The task was to make a fruit pie, and Gina had used Gram's recipe with the cream cheese filling. It was totally out of Gina's realm, and the consistency hadn't come out great.

Gina glanced at Bronwyn as the judges forked up pieces of each of their pies and whispered to each other. She couldn't tell, but she thought Pia made a sour face when she bit into Gina's. Bronwyn was staring straight ahead at the judges, the tension radiating off her.

Gina wanted to win, to prove to herself that she wasn't without skills, as Hugh had always implied, but hadn't she already proven that? The prize money would come in handy for the motel, but Bronwyn had a much more important reason to want the prize money.

The judges put down their forks, and Hogan Fillery spoke. "Gina, your pie has a certain unique flavor, but the consistency leaves a lot to be desired. Bronwyn, your pie brings back fond childhood memories, and the consistency is perfect." He paused dramatically. "Bronwyn, you are the winner!"

Bronwyn let out a breath, her expression incredulous as she turned to Gina. Gina high-fived her. The crowd cheered.

Bronwyn gave Gina a hug before heading up to the judge's table to accept her trophy and the check. "You did great, Gina. I'm sorry you didn't win."

"I'm not sorry. Congratulations." Gina couldn't be happier with the outcome of the contest.

Jules and Maddie joined her as she cleaned up her area.

"You did such a great job," Maddie gushed.

"Sorry you didn't win," Jules said.

"I'm kind of glad Bronwyn won. She needed the money for her grandmother," Gina said. "I know we could use the money for the motel, too, but I think this whole thing was a big win overall. We proved that people are welcome back to Shell Cove."

"We did. And when the show airs on TV, more of them will come, at least for a while." Maddie looked a bit stressed for a second, but then she brightened. "I say we celebrate with coffees from Ocean Brew."

Gina felt better than she had in a long time as she joined her cousins at Ocean Brew. The divorce and all the self-doubt had taken its toll, but her time in Shell Cove had been therapeutic. For the first time in a long time, she felt like she belonged. Shell Cove was a beautiful town with great people, and it didn't hurt that Cassie knew exactly how to make a latte just the way she liked it.

She turned from the counter with hers in hand and noticed Nick Barlowe coming in the door, his gaze pinned on Jules as he came toward them.

"I think someone might want to talk to you." Gina jutted her chin toward Nick.

Jules frowned. "Who?" She turned just as Nick reached them.

"Hi, Jules." Nick sounded nervous. He half smiled at Gina and Maddie.

"Hi," Jules said.

The two of them stood there staring at each other. Gina could feel the tension and the attraction between the two of them.

"Can I talk to you?" Nick asked Jules.

Clearly he meant alone, so Gina took Maddie's arm and pulled her away. "Let's go sit on the bench across from Saltwater Sweets and watch them make chocolate. We'll catch you later, Jules."

CHAPTER FORTY-TWO

*J*ules stirred another packet of sugar into her coffee and watched the steam swirl up. Nick had suggested they sit in the corner booth, and she was brimming with curiosity over what he wanted to talk to her about. It reminded her of the day they'd sat in there talking about themselves. She'd felt a connection that day. Maybe things weren't ruined between them.

"I'm sorry I got testy at the bank the other day and acted like a snob the other night when we were having ice cream." Jules figured she would get that out of the way. She was embarrassed that she'd acted like a spoiled child. "I'm not usually prone to dramatics like that."

Nick's smile lit his face, and she couldn't help but smile herself. "I'm the one who should be apologizing."

"You already did." Jules looked at him from underneath her lashes. "So maybe we should forget all about it. As it turns out, getting the occupancy permit was actually a good thing because we needed it to rent the rooms to the baking show."

"I'd like that." Nick put a stack of papers on the table between them.

"What's that?"

He pushed the papers toward her. "It's the loan for the Beachcomber. You and your cousins just need to look it over and sign in the appropriate spots. If you have formed a business entity, write that in and initial."

Jules stared down at the paperwork. She'd actually been a little disappointed that Gina had lost the contest. That prize money would have come in handy at the Beachcomber. Even though Maddie was making it sound like they were doing okay, she knew that with the baking contest crew leaving, there wouldn't be much money coming in until the show aired and brought a trickle of tourists, but even that wouldn't be forever.

"You mean the bank approved it?"

"Yep. I worked it out with the main branch."

Jules stared at him. She had a feeling that he'd had to jump through some hoops to work it out. "What about your grandfather?"

"It turns out he's all for it."

"Seriously? This is awesome." Jules thumbed

through the papers. Now she knew for sure she was right where she was supposed to be.

Jules looked out the window to see Rose, Pearl, and Leena walking past.

They were with Nick's grandfather, talking and laughing.

"Your grandfather does seem happier lately," Jules said.

Nick's gaze followed the old man, and Jules could see how much Nick loved him reflected in his eyes. "He sure does."

"I wonder if it has something to do with that letter," Jules mused.

"Letter?"

"We found an envelope in Gram's things. It was addressed to your grandfather, but she never sent it. Rose gave it to him."

Nick's eyebrows rose. "Really? Interesting. He didn't mention anything about a letter. Maybe that explains his recent happiness. What did it say?"

Jules shrugged. "No idea. It was sealed."

Nick glanced out at his grandfather just as the four seniors burst out laughing. "Well, whatever it was, it seems to have done him a world of good."

Jules straightened the loan papers into a neat pile in front of her. "I'm sure my cousins will be happy to sign this, but we'll probably run it by Gram's lawyer first."

"Sure, no problem." Nick hesitated, seeming nervous. "Maybe once it's signed, I could take you to dinner to celebrate."

Jules smiled. "I think I'd like that."

CHAPTER FORTY-THREE

"You did great!" Rose hugged Gina, almost causing her to spill her coffee. "Imagine lasting to the final round."

"I knew you could master baking pies just like your grandmother." Pearl winked at Gina.

"Be careful what you wish for. Now everyone will be expecting you to bring fabulous pies to the town potluck events," Leena said.

"Well, who knows if I can keep that up?" Gina grimaced. "Some of those wins were just luck. Andy burned his crust, and Brad was distracted."

Gina was shrugging off the praise, but Maddie could tell she was secretly pleased.

"And look at how the town has been transformed." Rose gestured toward the groups of tourists who were milling about. The town did look a lot better. It was more inviting with its fresh paint, flowers, and new awnings. The shops seemed brighter, too, and the tourists strolling along with colorful shopping bags added to the bustling vibe.

"The baking contest really did bring a lot of people here. It's been amazing, and we have a few reservations for next week at the motel. It's definitely brought awareness of our town, but I'm not sure it will last," Maddie said.

"Oh, it won't." Rose sat down next to her on the bench. "We need to create a buzz about the town. Give tourists a reason to come here."

"We kind of lucked out with the baking contest, but now we need to be more deliberate," Pearl said.

Pearl and Rose exchanged a glance.

"What do you mean? What's going on?" Maddie asked.

The ladies were clearly holding back about something.

"We need to take specific action," Pearl said.

"And we need a specific person to take that action," Leena added.

Rose turned to Maddie. "And that person is you. We've spoken to the mayor, and he's agreed to open up the chamber of commerce position again. We want you to fill it."

Maddie didn't know what to say. She was busy at the motel, but the new position was intriguing. "What does that entail? I do have responsibilities at the motel."

"Don't worry about that. It's just part time. You can manage the motel and head the chamber of commerce, but you'd have more clout with the chamber of commerce title," Pearl said.

"And a budget." Leena rubbed her forefinger and thumb together.

"Don't get too excited about the budget though. It's only a small sum from the permit fees that the baking show paid. But you'll be able to use it for advertising and setting things up," Rose said. "So basically you just need to organize the town events. Reaching out to vendors and putting ads in papers will go smoother with your new title. What do you say?"

Maddie mulled it over. She did still have the Beach-comber to think about, but she had all the renovation projects mapped out and organized. Running the motel wasn't that hard, and Jules and Gina would help. She would have some extra time, and the truth was she had to come up with ways to bring people to Shell Cove anyway. That would make it easier.

"Okay, I'll do it," she said.

"Great!" Rose clapped. "I'll set up a meeting for next month, and you can present your ideas."

Maddie panicked. "Wait. Next month? That's kind of soon. Isn't it?"

Rose fixed her with a serious look. "We need to keep

the tourists flowing. If we don't, the shop owners are going to get discouraged, and things will go back to the way they were. You don't want that, do you?"

"No, of course not. I'm sure I can come up with something by then." Maddie wasn't at all sure, but at least she could try. But since it seemed like she would be staying in Shell Cove, she had something else on her mind. "There is one thing that might help me."

"What is it?"

"That cottage on the beach, Starfish Cottage? Do you think you could help persuade the bank to sell it to me and give me a loan?"

The three ladies smiled at each other. "I think we can. It just so happens we have an old friend in high places over there."

AFTER GINA AND MADDIE LEFT TO WINDOW-SHOP, Rose, Pearl, and Leena stayed on the bench enjoying the activity on the street. It was still early summer, but the day had been a scorcher. The cool ocean breeze made it pleasant.

"It's so nice to have people here again!" Rose took a deep breath and committed the feelings, sights, and sounds to memory. She wanted to relive it just in case tourists dried up and they couldn't bring them back. It wasn't that she didn't have confidence in Maddie. She did, but at her age, she knew better than to count her chickens before they hatched.

"Get your wallet out, Leena. It looks like Rose and I are going to win the Nules bet," Pearl said.

Leena frowned. "Nules?"

"Yeah, Nick and Jules." Pearl nodded toward Ocean Brew, where Jules and Nick were seated at a table by the window and looking very chummy.

Leena made a show of craning her neck to assess the situation. "They're just having coffee. I don't think it's a date. They have paperwork in front of them."

"Maybe it's the loan," Rose said. "I was hoping Henry would see the light on that."

"Never mind Henry. I think that Nick did that on his own," Pearl said.

"Even better." Rose turned to Leena. "Maybe it is too soon, but judging by the way those two are looking at each other, you're going to lose this bet."

"I don't think you'll win the Chukeena bet either." Pearl nodded toward Saltwater Sweets.

"Let me guess. That's Chuck and Deena?" Leena said.

"Yep. They look very lovey-dovey in there."

Leena made a sour face. "Who has time for that at her age?"

"What? You don't think about getting married again?" Rose asked.

Leena was divorced. Rose and Pearl were widows.

Rose had never heard either of her friends voice any desire to be married, but they were quite a bit older than Deena.

"No. Why would I? I love being independent and not having to compromise. What about you?" Leena asked Rose.

Rose contemplated the idea. She never felt lonely, mostly because her grandson, Dex, doted on her. She didn't think she would have room for a man in her life. "I don't think so. I like things the way they are."

"Well, I would," Pearl said.

Rose and Leena looked at her in surprise.

"You would?" Leena asked. "Huh, maybe we should think of someone to fix you up with. How about Henry? He's being so nice to us now, and he really is a good guy."

Pearl looked shocked. "Henry? No! He's an old friend, almost like a brother. Besides, I can find my own man, thank you."

"Well darn, I was hoping to have another couple to bet on," Leena said.

"What about Maddie and Dex?" Pearl suggested. "I'd put money on those two getting together."

Leena made a face. "Are you kidding? They're complete opposites. Besides, Dex has that horrid girlfriend."

"Lorelie." Rose wrinkled her nose. Rose didn't much care for Dex's girlfriend. She was shallow and selfish, and she talked negatively about Shell Cove. She'd been trying to convince Dex to move to Portland, where she lived, and Rose was afraid she might succeed. Dex always said that he loved Shell Cove, but that girl could be persuasive. She would miss Dex terribly if he moved, but more importantly, she feared his life would be miserable if he made more permanent arrangements with the girl. "I'd rather see him with Maddie. I wonder if that can be arranged."

"It's possible." Pearl's gaze was following Gina, who was across the street looking into one of the empty shops. "I think there are a few things that can be arranged here. If you'll excuse me, I'm going to tend to one of them now."

GINA'S FINGER HOVERED OVER THE SEND BUTTON ON HER phone. She'd just written a message to her friend, Melissa, and once she sent it, there would be no going back. She stared down at the words.

You can stop looking for property. I'm staying in Shell Cove.

Was she doing the right thing?

Looking out over the town, she saw something much different from what she'd seen when she first arrived. Main Street was bustling with activity, the stores brightly lit and welcoming, the flowers blooming. The ocean to the east was awash in gorgeous hues of blue and pink, a reflection of the sun setting behind her.

From her vantage point, she could see a section of the pier, which made her think of the pie contest. That contest was what had brought people to town, and her work helping her cousins on the motel had made the motel inviting for them to stay in. It was the first time she'd done something bigger than herself, something with a purpose.

She pressed Send.

"I hope you're thinking about your next pie. You're going to need one for the meeting in a few weeks when Maddie tells us all about her great ideas." Pearl had apparently crossed the street while Gina was typing and was standing beside her. "Of course, there will be a potluck."

"I think I can come up with something." Gina felt confident, a new and welcome feeling for her.

"I'm sure you'll do something fantastic. Your grand-mother said you had potential."

"She did?" Gina was touched. "I miss her."

"We all do." Pearl glanced into the empty store they were standing in front of. "You know, this empty store used to be a bakery. They had the most delicious cream horns. It would make a great pie shop. I think every-thing is still in there."

They cupped their hands over their eyes and pressed them against the glass to get a better look at the interior.

It appeared to be in good condition. Rich, honey-colored wide-pine flooring led to a row of glass cases. The cases still had their shelves, and the glass gleamed. In one corner, chairs were stacked on top of square tables. Gina imagined the back room would have a commercial refrigerator, ovens, and stainless steel counters, everything one needed to make pies, but her confidence wasn't quite at that level. "I don't think I'm ready to start up a pie baking business yet. I can barely get one pie done in an hour, never mind dozens."

Pearl nodded. "It would be the perfect place when you are."

The idea had potential. It was something she could work toward. Hugh would laugh at her if he knew she was aspiring to be a pie maker, but she no longer cared what Hugh thought. Sure, making pies in Shell Cove was a far cry from the fancy committees and luncheons she'd had in the city, but her new kind of life was more appealing.

"I'll need to build up to it. Maybe I can practice in the Beachcomber kitchen."

"Oh! That could be a good hook for guests. Fresh-baked pies! What motel does that?" Pearl looked pleased. "I think you might be on to something."

"That's not a bad idea. I'll mention it to Maddie."

"So, you're staying in Shell Cove, then? It's not quite as exciting as Boston."

Gina looked out over the town, a smile tugging at

her lips. "No, but it has its charms. Life here is simpler, and I think I'm ready for that."

As Gina parted ways with Pearl, she felt content. She'd fulfilled her promise to Gram, and it turned out Gram had been wiser than she'd thought. The simple things were better.

CHAPTER FORTY-FOUR

*J*ules, Maddie, and Gina stood in the driveway and waved to Marilyn as she drove off. All the baking contest people had left earlier. They'd assured the cousins that they'd loved their stay at the Beachcomber.

"I say things have improved a lot since we first laid eyes on this place," Maddie said.

Jules glanced at the fresh paint, the new plants, and the fixed porch. The motel still needed work, but it looked so much better. "And now that we have the loan, we'll be able to get this place into tip-top shape."

Jules thought of her grandmother. They were going to fulfill the wish in her will that they make the Beachcomber profitable again. But even more importantly, Jules had proved to herself that she *could* run a motel again. Even working with Gina and Maddie didn't seem so bad. In fact, she was looking forward to it.

"Everything worked out great. Except now we have rooms to clean." Gina made a face.

"And pies to practice," Maddie teased.

Gina had mentioned the empty bakery downtown and that she wasn't ready for that much of a commitment. She needed more practice.

Jules thought it was a fantastic idea for her to practice baking pies at the motel. "Imagine how enticing it will be for the guests to smell fresh-baked pie in the lobby. That's something folks will talk about when they get back home and a unique selling proposition for the motel."

"*If* we get more guests," Gina pointed out.

"We have a few rooms booked, and when the baking show airs on TV, more will come." Maddie sounded optimistic.

"And when you come up with another event that will bring people to town once the interest from the baking show dries up, we'll have more tourists," Jules said to Maddie.

Maddie looked a bit nervous, but before she could say anything, an old Honda Accord with a variety of dings and a faded gray paint job swerved into a parking spot and belched out a puff of smoke.

A colorfully dressed woman who looked to be in her late seventies hopped out. She stretched and took a deep breath. "Hello there! I suppose I'm too late for the baking contest?"

"Are you Aggie?" Jules asked.

"Yes indeed! Aggie Fletcher. Do you gals run the place?"

"We do." Jules felt a sense of relief as she introduced her cousins.

Marilyn had mentioned she'd never heard from Aggie, and they'd all been worried.

"Where have you been? We thought you got lost," Maddie said.

Aggie gestured toward the car. "Old Bessie broke down a few hours south of here! Lucky thing a nice young couple picked me up on the side of the road. I had to have it fixed. It all turned out good, though. I stayed at a wonderful inn called Tides. It's in Lobster Bay. It was just so lovely that I guess I lost track of time. The inn was on the beach, and they had an adorable golden retriever named Cooper. Such fun! And they have the cutest bakery in town called Sandcastles."

Jules smiled at Aggie's bubbly memories of Lobster Bay. Jules herself had fond memories of the town and of Sandcastles bakery with its sandcastle-shaped cakes and exceptionally delicious pastries. "I used to live in Lobster Bay. I love the Sandcastle's cakes."

"Yes! Quite unique. Anyway it was so much fun there that I decided to stay awhile. I made some new friends. It took a while to fix the car. I should trade it in.

I saw a cute red sportster at the used-car lot here in town. Maybe I'll go for that!"

"Marilyn was worried when you didn't show up. She kept calling but never got in touch with you," Maddie said.

"Oh, dear me. I didn't mean to worry anyone. I turned off my phone. My son can be a worrywart. He was bothering me with constant calls. I don't like to have my style cramped. I wouldn't have made the contest in time because the car wasn't ready, so I left a message for Marilyn. Didn't she get it?"

Jules shook her head. "No. She said she never heard from you."

"Oh my, hopefully I didn't send the message to the wrong number like before." Aggie squinted at the phone screen then shrugged and put the phone away. "Oh well, water under the bridge now! So, who won the contest?"

"Bronwyn Saunders," Gina said, omitting the whole story about how she had filled in for Aggie. Jules wondered if she should say something but figured she would leave it to her cousin.

"Oh, good! She's a nice kid. She deserves a win." Aggie showed no disappointment in having to forfeit her spot in the competition. "I am sorry I missed it, but it's lovely here and much nicer to stay when I don't have to work at baking. You wouldn't happen to have an extra room available, would you?"

Maddie smiled. "As a matter of fact, we have one ready and waiting just for you."

Jules checked Aggie in. They were getting into a routine, with each of them having their own responsibilities. Jules's job was to deal with the check-ins. She liked interacting with the people, but once the motel was getting more guests, she would need to hire some help.

When she was done, Maddie pulled a bottle of pinot noir out of the fridge and suggested they sit on the porch and drink to the successes of the past week.

"It looks like Gram knew what she was doing when she left us this motel," Maddie said once they were settled in their porch chairs.

"She would be proud at what we've accomplished in such a short time," Jules agreed.

"It's not quite as dilapidated as it was when we first came, but we still have a ways to go." Gina glanced behind her at the building. It did still need some paint, new gutters, and other repairs, but Jules could tell that even Gina was pleased with their progress.

"We do," Jules said. "But I feel like this is just the beginning for the Beachcomber and the entire town of Shell Cove."

Maddie tilted her wineglass toward her cousins, and they clinked rims. "And the beginning for each of us too."

. . .

****

I HOPE YOU ENJOYED YOUR VISIT TO SHELL COVE. There are a lot more stories to tell in this town. Maddie's is next. Will she get her dream cottage and find another great event to bring to town? Find out in book 2 **STARFISH COTTAGE**:

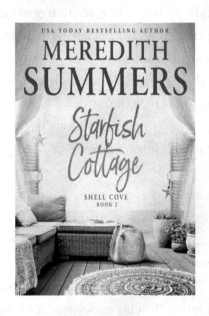

JOIN MY NEWSLETTER FOR SNEAK PEEKS OF MY LATEST books and release day notifications:
  https://lobsterbay1.gr8.com

These fabulous pie recipes are courtesy of retired food columnist Paula Anderson, in Scarborough, Maine, and Hobe Sound, in Florida. Thank you, Paula!

NEVER FAIL FOOD PROCESSOR PIE CRUST

Gina had a problem with her first few attempts at pie crust. Too bad she didn't have this recipe!

<u>Ingredients:</u>

3 cups all-purpose flour

1/2 cup well-chilled solid vegetable shortening, cubed

1/2 cup well-chilled unsalted butter, cubed

3/4 Tbsp. salt

1/3 cup plus 1 Tbsp. ice water, or as needed

Directions:

Pulse flour, shortening, butter, and salt in a food processor in one-second bursts or until shortening and butter are the size of peas.

With motor running, pour ice water through feed tube slowly and steadily, adding just enough to moisten. The mixture should just start to hold together but still look crumbly. (NOTE: making crust in food processor usually requires less water than other recipes.)

Pour mixture into a bowl. Gather into a ball with your hands, smooshing to make it stick together. Divide in half and shape into two flat discs and wrap each in plastic wrap. Refrigerate at least thirty minutes or up to twenty-four hours. (NOTE: can also freeze up to three months.) Roll out each disc into a twelve-inch circle and use in your favorite recipe.

For single-crust pies with unbaked filling: Transfer dough to a pie plate, and trim excess on edge to about one inch. Roll under and pinch or crimp as desired. Using a fork, prick sides and bottom, then chill ten minutes in freezer before baking. Line crust with foil, and add pie weights if desired. Bake in a preheated 450°F oven for eight minutes. Remove foil and pie weights, and bake until golden brown, about six or seven minutes. Cool before filling.

For pies with baked filling: Transfer dough to a pie plate and fill pie. (Mound generously if using fruit because it shrinks a lot.) Lay top crust (if using) over filling and pinch both doughs together to seal. Trim excess on edge to about one inch. Roll under and pinch or crimp as desired. If using a top crust, cut a few slits in the top, then chill ten minutes in freezer before baking. Bake in a preheated 450°F oven fifteen minutes. Lower oven temperature to 375°F, and bake until filling is bubbly and pie crust is golden brown, about forty to forty-five minutes.

OREO COOKIE PIE CRUST

Ingredients:

Makes one (nine-inch) crust, eight servings.

18 OREO Cookies. (If you're like me, you'll need a lot more than eighteen because you'll eat half of them.)

3 Tbsp. butter, melted

Directions:

Place cookies in a large Ziploc bag and seal. Use rolling pin to crush cookies to form fine crumbs.

Add butter. Squeeze bag to evenly moisten crumbs.

Press crumb mixture onto bottom and up side of nine-inch pie plate sprayed with nonstick cooking spray. Refrigerate until ready to fill.

QUICK AND YUMMY STRAWBERRY PIE
(Adapted from Kraft Foods)

This one didn't come out so great when Gina made it for the town meeting. Yours will come out just perfect, though.

Ingredients:

2 cups fresh strawberries, rinsed, hulled, and divided
2/3 cup boiling water
1 pkg. (3 oz.) Jell-O strawberry-flavored gelatin
ice cubes
1/2 cup cold water

1 tub (8 oz.) nondairy whipped topping, thawed according to directions (like Cool Whip)

1 (9-inch pie) pie crust, prebaked and cooled (may substitute graham cracker crust or chocolate cookie crust)

Directions:

Slice one cup strawberries. Refrigerate for later use. Chop remaining strawberries in 1/4 inch slices. Set aside.

Add boiling water to gelatin mix. Stir two minutes or until completely dissolved. Add enough ice to the 1/2 cup of cold water to measure one cup. Add to gelatin. Stir until slightly thickened. Remove any unmelted ice.

Whisk in whipped topping then stir in chopped strawberries. Refrigerate thirty to forty minutes or until mixture is very thick and will mound on a spoon. Spoon into prepared crust.

Refrigerate six hours or until firm. Decorate top with sliced berries just before serving.

MEEMA'S SPECIAL APPLE PIE

FOR THE CRUST:

1 3/4 cups all-purpose flour

1/4 cup sugar

1 tsp. cinnamon

1/4 tsp. salt

10 Tbsp. unsalted butter

1/4 cup very cold apple juice

FOR THE FILLING:

1 2/3 cup sour cream

1 cup sugar

1/3 cup all-purpose flour

1 large egg, beaten

2 tsp. vanilla

1/4 tsp. salt

8 Granny Smith apples, peeled, cored, and thinly sliced

FOR THE TOPPING:

1/2 cup all-purpose flour

1/3 cup sugar

1/3 cup firmly packed light-brown sugar

1 Tbsp. cinnamon

Dash salt

8 Tbsp. unsalted butter, softened

1 cup chopped walnuts

Directions:

To prepare crust: Combine flour, sugar, cinnamon, and salt in medium bowl. Cut in butter until mixture resembles coarse meal. Add apple juice and toss mixture gently with a fork until evenly moistened. Gather dough into a ball. Transfer to a lightly floured surface. Roll dough into a circle slightly larger than a deep ten-inch pie plate. Fit pastry into pan, and flute with a high edge. Set aside.

To prepare filling: Combine sour cream, sugar, flour, egg, vanilla, and salt in a large bowl. Mix well. Fold in apple slices. Spoon mixture into pastry-lined pie plate. Bake ten minutes in a preheated 450°F oven. Reduce oven temperature to 350°F and continue baking forty minutes or until filling is puffed and golden brown.

To prepare topping: Meanwhile, combine flour, both sugars, cinnamon, and salt in a medium bowl. Mix well. Blend in butter, mashing with a fork, until mixture is crumbly. Add nuts and mix well. Spoon over cooked pie. Return to oven and bake for fifteen minutes. Cool completely and cut.

ABOUT THE AUTHOR

Meredith Summers writes cozy mysteries as USA Today Bestselling author Leighann Dobbs and crime fiction as L. A. Dobbs.

She spent her childhood summers in Ogunquit Maine and never forgot the soft soothing feeling of the beach. She hopes to share that feeling with you through her books which are all light, feel-good reads.

Join her newsletter for sneak peeks of the latest books and release day notifications:

https://lobsterbay1.gr8.com

This is a work of fiction.

None of it is real. All names, places, and events are products of the author's imagination. Any resemblance to real names, places, or events are purely coincidental, and should not be construed as being real.

BEACHCOMBER MOTEL

Copyright © 2021

Meredith Summers

http://www.meredithsummers.com

All Rights Reserved.

No part of this work may be used or reproduced in any manner, except as allowable under "fair use," without the express written permission of the author.

❋ Created with Vellum